Maieman Paradox Book I
D.L. Hannah

ISBN 9781965798287   2026

Contents

Isis: We have our FOURTH series, baby! Mama is tired!

Chapter 1

Queen Marietta's past

Marietta Daynes held the tiny baby in her arms, in awe of her beauty.

"She looks just like her mother!" she whispered.

Inhaling her sweet, sugary scent, she carefully wrapped the sapphire-toned blanket around her while humming a soft tune. "What is her name, Your Majesty?"

King Carlomon looked as if he hadn't slept in days. She suspected he hadn't.

"My daughter named her Princess Revari Ava Amorous." He grimaced. "Of course, I've changed it to Carogue now. I don't want my granddaughters to be associated with any part of King Dubian's family."

Gently rocking the baby, she said, "I understand. It's all so—" Her eyes filled with tears. "—so terrible! To lose Queen Dellah this way! I don't understand any of it."

His sad eyes swept over her. "I understand how you feel. She was so young. Had I known Dubian was insane, I never would've

1

agreed to the marriage." He sighed. "I blame myself, but what's done is done. I hope I can make it up to her by rearing her daughters the way she'd want."

"If there's anything I can do to help—" said Marietta.

"We don't need your assistance," said a crisp, unfriendly voice.

King Carlomon stood. "Opal! I didn't expect you to awaken so soon."

Princess Opal tried to remove Princess Revari from Marietta's arms. For a split second, Marietta resisted, then gave the baby to her.

"I've slept long enough. I woke up to check on Vivant, and now," she said, righting the baby in her arms, "I want to see how this little blessing is doing."

She tossed a dismissive look toward Marietta. "You've seen the princesses. I'm sure you have other things to do back on Seng?"

"Opal, Marietta and Dellah were friends. Please don't be rude."

"I wouldn't know who was my sister's friend and who wasn't. You sent me to Earth, remember?" Casting a critical eye at Marietta's prim clothing, she said, "I'm surprised Dellah would befriend someone belonging to a class beneath us."

Marietta decided she'd had quite enough of Princess Opal's disrespect. She secretly applauded King Carlomon for getting her out of the way after she murdered innocent ChildForms. Marietta hadn't missed her, nor had Dellah mentioned her since she'd been gone.

Wrapping an expensive silk cloth around her head, she said, "Thank you for allowing me to visit with the princesses, Your Highness. I'm not looking forward to Queen Dellah's DeathCeremony, but I'd be a poor friend if I didn't attend."

King Carlomon grasped both of her hands in his. "You're always welcome in my palace. I'm just sorry it had to be at such a sad occasion."

She bowed to him before halfheartedly bowing to Princess Opal. "In a while, Your Majesties."

"What kind of WomanForm pilots crafts?" she heard the princess say when she passed through the palace's massive gates.

She adjusted the controls, lifted her craft into the air, and prayed for the princesses and King Carlomon to live a long and prosperous life.

Although she knew it was wrong to wish Princess Opal had died instead of her friend, it didn't change how she felt. Queen Dellah's daughters were now in the hands of a sick mind. She hoped The One would spare them from her madness.

Several years later

King Micah disconnected the transmission from his TeleScreen, rubbing his weary eyes.

"Micah? Are you ready for breakfast?"

He turned to her with his hand outstretched. "Come here, my dear."

She entered the bed chamber and took his hand. "What is it?"

"Princess Opal is dead. One of her soldiers cut her throat."

"By The One! And what of the princesses?"

"They'll be staying with their father."

She rested her forehead on his shoulder. "Oh no! First, we lost Dellah, then Coldarius. Now this? Micah, those ChildForms will go through hell if they stay with him! Especially Princess Revari. She's so young."

He brushed the back of his hand across her cheek. "That's true, but what can we do? He's Platirius's king and...his power has grown since he defeated King Hitam."

"For a brief moment, I went out of my mind when I held Revari in my arms. I thought about taking her out of King Carlomon's palace. Just...running with her and never looking back. But I knew it wouldn't have happened. I would've been executed."

His thumb caressed the back of her hand. "I'm glad you thought better of it."

"I wouldn't have been able to give her a life. I hadn't met you yet. But now," she said, looking around, "we could give them a wonderful home—here with our sons!"

"King Dubian would raze Maieman to the ground before he let that happen. I hate it just as much as you, but there's nothing we can do for them now."

"But I have to stay in their lives! Dellah would've wanted me to!"

"We can only get as close to them as their father will allow us to." He shook his head in disgust. "You know he's out of his mind, Marietta."

"I know. That's what scares me!"

"Come. Let us go to breakfast. Things will work out in the end."

Queen Marietta tried to convince herself that her husband was right, but she couldn't shake the feeling that things could go wrong. Terribly wrong.

The present

"My Queen, King Jonah is here."

Queen Revari looked out the window as the king descended from his craft, following a handful of soldiers.

A frown clouded her beautiful face. "What does he want?"

"Shall I go to him, My Queen?"

"No. Let him come. If he annoys me, I'll send him on his way. Make sure his soldiers stay outside in the rain."

"Yes, Queen Revari."

After a few minutes, the TeleShield buzzed.

"Come in," she called.

He entered and stopped at the sight of her. Propped up on pillows, she sat on a plump red divan, scantily clad in a red night robe. Matching fuzzy, high-heeled slippers lay close by.

Two manicurists concentrated on polishing her fingernails. The silky red polish reminded him of blood. When she crossed her legs, he noticed her tiny toes had already been polished.

"How can I help you, King Jonah?"

She was so beautiful, he almost forgot what he'd come to say.

"Yes?" she asked impatiently.

He cleared his throat. "You knew this day was coming, didn't you?"

She rolled her eyes. "I'm in no mood for riddles. I'd appreciate if you'd tell me what the hell you want, then leave my palace."

He circled the divan to stand in front of her. "King Anemi may have killed my brother, but you set him on a course to his death. If it weren't for the drug you spiked in his drink, he would've been strong enough to defeat your grandfather."

She pursed her lips. "Maybe he would have and maybe he wouldn't." She uncrossed her ankles. "But we'll never know, will we?"

A manicurist sprayed *Visinite* on her nails to instantly dry the polish to an immaculate finish.

Stretching out her leg to peruse her pretty toes, she said, "If you've come to address my past sins, save it. General Kron is dead and he's not coming back. Don't look so glum," she said as she put on her slippers. "If you die, you can have a nice family reunion in Hell."

His strong hand gripped the top of the divan. "What a wicked WomanForm you've become!"

Laughing, she accepted a glass of wine from one of the staff and raised it high in the air. "Thank you!"

"What happened to you, Revari? You used to be so kind and thoughtful."

She took a sip of the sweet PotterBerry wine. "It's Queen Revari. We're not friends. And to answer your idiotic question, King Dubian happened."

"But he's dead. How long will his ghost haunt you?"

She found that hysterically entertaining.

"You're asking me? Aren't you standing in front of me, pouting over a ghost?"

"You had no right to hurt Lucian! He was coming home to see us. You can't imagine how much my parents and I missed him. Do you have any idea what you took from us?"

"You mean what King Anemi took from you. I'm not the one who smothered him to death!"

"No, you just drugged him so he couldn't fight back!" he shouted.

The glass was set down before he had a chance to blink. She signaled for the staff to go.

"I don't allow MaleForms to raise their voices to me."

Her tone was soft. Deadly.

"I grew tired of listening to King Dubian rant and rave about me killing my mother and how he wished I had died instead of her. Loud voices...vex me. I'll say this only once: Leave my halls. Now."

"Or what? You'll kill me like you tried to kill Lucian?"

A red glow slowly formed in her eyes. "If that's what you came here asking for, who am I to deny your request? Here you stand, barking like a wounded puppy over a MaleForm I despise just a bit less than my father. I heard you never wanted to be king. I'll gladly put you out of your misery and take over Maieman."

Her chilling, blank stare swept over him. "Due to her friendship with my mother, Queen Marietta's life will be spared. But you have no such recourse."

"What happened to my friend?" he asked.

"We were friends? Funny, I don't remember. Let's see... She was beaten, went to bed without supper, and after her family was murdered, she was locked away for several years."

Closing his eyes, he bowed his head.

"I think she died in the Chamber of Despair," she whispered.

"Don't say that," he begged. "Don't say it as if you're past all hope!"

She chuckled mirthlessly. "You should see someone at your wellness chamber. Clearly, you have issues with letting go of the past."

"So do you."

"Maybe, but I don't go barging into places where I'm not welcome. Final warning. Go."

He reached the door, then stopped. "There was a time when you would've asked me to stay. You've forgotten all the good times we had."

"I have," she said. "Whatever memories you're holding on to didn't help me while I was locked up. You weren't there to help me either, so you have no right to barge into my home and pass judgment on me. Not everyone can be a good, pure soul like you."

"You know nothing about my soul. You've forgotten everything that matters."

"The only thing that matters to me is my son, my sister and nieces, and the family I've built—my Revaltians. Nothing else warrants my attention."

"That's not true. My family has loved you your whole life."

She cocked her head. "A life I no longer care to remember, King Jonah. In a while."

He turned and paused at the door. "Before your father blew your life to hell, you were different. We played and shared our meals together. Your mother restored some of your memories, but not all of them."

Her tone was curt and final. "I have the ones I need to remember."

He shook his head. "No, you don't! You don't remember what our friendship meant to each other!"

"Why do you think I'd want to? Admit you want to avenge General Kron and leave. Your little games won't work on me."

He smacked a wall, causing a painting of her late husband to rattle. "That's the problem with you! You always think someone is out to get you!"

She took a step toward him. "First, keep your hands off my walls. Second, you show up here dripping with indignation, wanting me to take a twisted ride down memory lane. Do you expect me not to be on guard? I don't trust MaleForms!"

He matched her step. "What about Gallium? Or King Justin? Do you trust them?"

"They're my family," she sneered. "What are you to me?"

He gazed at her for a long moment. "Had you not gone to Earth, that Human would've never become linked to you. You would've been *my* wife—the one who would've known exactly who and what I am. Yet, there you stand, so cold and unbothered!"

She took a step backward when he reached for her.

"It's all right to show emotion. It's not a crime!"

"Trespassing is. Since I've asked you to leave and you're still standing there breathing my air, I could have my Revaltians throw you out of here on your ass. I won't tell you again."

"Fine, I'm leaving." He noted her BrainStaffs hanging above her desk. Before she took half of Platirius's throne, no WomanForm had earned them. "I didn't realize I'd made peace with what you did until I saw you again. You still steal the air out of my lungs. I wish—"

Her eyebrow rose. "You wish what?"

"It does no good to say anything more. Not now at least."

"Perhaps never."

"No. You had a good life before you went to Earth. You were loved and supported. If only you had come to me that night instead of going to that desolate place!"

"If I had, what would you have done?"

"I would've protected you!"

"Vivant worked with my father to bring me back. You've tried to move heaven and Maieman for her for years. What would make me believe you'd ever betray her?"

"Nothing I did was for her, Revari. It was all for you."

He turned and buzzed his hand across the TeleShield, leaving her to reflect on his words.

King Asa's TeleScreen chirped on his nightstand. He groaned and rolled over. It was before dawn. The last thing he wanted was to talk. He slept very little whenever Queen Vivant visited. Not that he was complaining.

Her feminine prowess had him craving her soft skin long after she'd left for Platirius. The insistent chirping made him punch the air. He reached for it, grinding his teeth in annoyance before connecting the call.

"King Levi. This had better be important enough to disturb my rest!"

"How can anyone rest when a Human took over three realms and is controlling JanIus?! Why did you not stop him?"

King Asa sat up. "Who said it was my responsibility to stop him? I could ask you the same thing!"

"You could have ended him while he fought Queen Vivant! JanIus would've been yours and none of us would be in this mess!"

A hawk flew over a cluster of clouds covering a peek of the sun. Daybreak would arrive soon.

The darkness of his bed chamber hid King Asa's menacing scowl. "It's much too early for nonsense. What do you want?"

"I want that Human dead! Sooner rather than later! I've dispatched some of our most powerful kings to meet at my palace. Together, we'll devise a plan on how to destroy him. He owns three realms. We can't afford to have him attack one of us and earn another."

"I don't think his mind is on fighting and conquering."

"No? Is he not King Dubian's descendant? That's all he and his ruthless family have ever wanted—power! Let's not forget, if he comes for Platirius, there goes your chance of ruling it. Or have you forgotten since you've been dallying with Queen Vivant?"

King Asa gripped the TeleScreen. "I would advise you to keep your nose out of my business and your mouth off my lady before I cut both off your face. What I do and who I do it with doesn't concern you!"

"You not putting that Human out of his misery when you had the chance concerns all of us. Now we have to put our heads together and make things right!"

Thinking of the angel who had visited him, he said, "You weren't there. The realm of The One opened before my eyes. That means he didn't become king without His knowledge or permission. If you want to stand in His way, I won't stop you. I'm smart enough not to stoke His wrath!"

"No, I wasn't there, but as the treasurer of the Keeper of the Realms, I'll tell you where I will be—at my meeting. I expect you to be there."

The transmission disconnected. Swearing, King Asa threw off his bedcovers and headed for the bath chamber. A rooster crowed, signaling the beginning of the morning. He sighed when the hot stream of water hit his face.

The idea of a half-Human king didn't sit well with him either. Unlike King Levi, he had more to lose. His relationship with Queen Vivant and staying on The One's good side meant everything to him.

He'd planned to sit back and monitor King Justin from a distance until he found the right time to strike. Now, King Levi had upped the ante.

"Damn you, Levi!"

Years ago, the leaders of Platirius, Revani, Onzi, JanIus, and Maieman, had been officially appointed as the Keeper of the Realms by The One. They were responsible for overseeing the galaxy's affairs and keeping order within the realms.

True to his word, King Levi, the head treasurer, held a secret meeting in the recreation chamber of his palace. Over one thousand galactic kings were scattered about. Half of them visited the palace, while the rest, except for the Amorous sisters, King Asa, and King Justin, attended via TeleScreen.

After everyone had helped themselves to refreshments, he stood at the podium and waited for the noise to quiet down.

"I'll cut straight to the point. A Human has infiltrated our galaxy and has stolen three planets! The only time they were allowed here was for experimental research on Platirius. They aren't welcome in the galaxy! If you ask me, King Dubian should've never released Queen Revari from the Chamber of Despair."

His fist clenched into a tight ball. "She should still be rotting away for what she did!"

"Hear, hear!" someone shouted.

"I've reached out to King Asa, but he's been bewitched by Queen Vivant! I doubt he'll help us to rid ourselves of this perversion!"

King Abner raised his hand. "Now wait a minute. I've known Asa for a long time. I can assure you he's against the Human king too!"

He spread his hands in a circle. "If any of us were in his position—a step away from becoming Platirius's next king—would we jeopardize it for a Human? Asa might have a plan to eliminate him once he achieves his goal."

"We can't wait for him to decide what's to be done with the Human!" said King Levi. "We have to act now before he declares war on us."

King Asa entered the chamber. "No one asked you to wait on me," he said coldly.

"It's about time you arrived," said King Levi.

He pointed at King Levi. "I'll make this plain, I have my own plans for dealing with him. Stay out of my way."

King Levi raised a glass to him, smiling condescendingly.

King Abner motioned for King Asa to sit next to him.

"Has the Human mentioned attacking us?" asked King Jeroh.

"I don't know, Jeroh. I haven't sat down and had coffee with him!" said King Levi. "I heard he's appointed Gallium Barrios as his general."

King Marco stood. "And what do you think we can do against him? The story of him taking out the Old Kikhanians with a single breath isn't a myth! Queen Dellah made sure the battle was written in all of our Halls of Records. Without Gallium, we could easily kill him, but if we try, he'll end us all!"

"King Marco is right," said King Jeroh. "King Leighton was my friend. He struggled with inner demons like the rest of us, but he was a good king. I'm mad as hell that a Human is ruling his realm, but what can we do? We can't defeat him with Gallium!"

"Nor can we defeat Queen Vivant as long as she has Advisor TamRi and her sister's realm lining up with hers. Did that cross your mind or did you bring us here to eat your food?" asked King Marco.

King Levi looked at the laughing kings in horror. "You can't be serious! Are you saying we can't think of a way to eliminate one Human!"

"A Human who is protected by The One," said King Asa. "I don't speak for anyone except myself. I'm not crazy enough to anger Him. We've seen what happens when you go against His rules. King Belial and King Anemi should be all the cautionary tales we need to keep ourselves alive."

King Levi's eyes rolled back in his head. "He's just a Human. He's weaker than us—"

"I agree," said King Jeroh. "But I say the Human king should be left alone." He raised a hand in the air. "Don't misunderstand me! I don't want him here any more than you do! But mark my words, if we kill him, we'll be punished. If you're willing to try, go right ahead. I won't lift a finger to help!"

Another king stood. "Maybe we don't have to kill him. Perhaps we can make things so uncomfortable, he'll head back to Earth on his own."

King Levi adjusted his glasses on his nose. "What do you mean?"

"His mother brought him here after banishing him from Platirius. Maybe we can make her do it again."

"Explain."

"From what I heard, Platirius's old kings got inside his head and made him crazy. King Anemi might've been sent back to hell, but it's rumored the other evil Amorous spirits are there. If King Anemi got to him on JanIus, that means the others can too!"

King Levi stroked his beard. "Queen Vivant realizes he's a threat to her throne. She won't risk him forcing her WomenForms to submit to him."

The king nodded. "Precisely. All we have to do is make Queen Vivant think he's unbalanced enough to challenge her. Even Gallium won't be able to look the other way once the Human starts acting like King Dubian again.

It may force his hand to end him. He's a sworn enemy of the Amorous kings. Since we won't have a direct hand in killing him, we won't have to worry about The One's wrath falling upon us."

King Levi's shrewd eyes examined him like a specimen in a lab. "What's your stake in this?"

The king shrugged. "I have ambitions of my own. Ones that would be better served if King Justin is no longer around."

King Jeroh peered over his shoulder at King Asa. "But if King Asa takes JanIus, that'll give him enormous power. He could come for us any time he wants."

"I don't need JanIus to take your head, Jeroh. If you keep running your mouth, I don't mind killing you right here."

King Jeroh hastily turned away from him. Next to Platirius, King Asa had the largest realm and army. He was also the most vicious and cunning of the kings. None of his peers wanted to be his enemy.

King Levi waved his hand. "Let's not fight among ourselves. King Asa has always followed the rules. I'd rather him rule JanIus than a thieving Human."

All the kings surveyed each other, nodding their heads. It was a solid plan. The chance to rid themselves of the Human was so close they could taste it.

A jubilant King Levi dipped a shrimp into a small pot of sauce and popped it into his mouth. Things were looking up.

D omi stood in King Asa's enormous meeting chamber while he read a message on his TranScreen.

"Good news! You've been cleared for duty. You can report to Onyx when you're ready."

Onyx was the largest medical chamber on Onzi. It earned its name from the ingenious imagination of the architectural staff that had built it from pure onyx. Its beauty was second only to the majestic splendor of King Asa's palace.

Domi breathed a sigh of relief. She'd never been one to rest for long. Over time, the quiet solitude had begun to grate on her nerves.

"Thank you, Your Majesty," she said, bowing before him.

A hard slap to his muscular thigh made her jump. "I thought that would put a smile on your face! You'll meet with Colonel Chatz for training on Jeru. It's about an hour from here."

He closed the TranScreen. "He's expecting you, so don't be late."

"I won't, Your Majesty. And thank you for everything."

"Me? I haven't done anything. You, on the other hand, deserve this."

He stood and pinned a medal on her. "That's for demonstrating bravery and loyalty to my realm. I have to admit, I wasn't thrilled to have a female physician sent here, but if it had to be someone, I'm glad it was you."

She tried to blink back tears, but they spilled over.

"Come now," he said, rounding the desk to sit down. "Let us have none of that. I'm only telling the truth. You'll find a nice bonus in your account too. For the victory on Platirius and for taking care of...something foul that was polluting our galaxy."

Her heart sank as he stared at her.

"Nothing goes on in my kingdom without my knowing about it, Dominia. I meant what I said—you're one of mine now. Since I understand why you did it, I'm willing to keep your secret and protect you."

He partially stood when she sank to the floor. "What in the galaxy are you doing?!"

She wiped the sweat running from her curls down her face. "I thought I'd be killed if anyone found out!"

He sat back down. "Killing is necessary sometimes. Every part of Lady Alarah was evil. She had it coming for what she did to General Lyric."

He removed a small trinket from his desk and began flipping it between his fingers. "I told King Jonah and King Justin she went to Earth. As for Queen Vivant, I don't keep secrets from her. General Lyric was informed Lady Alarah is dead."

"What did General Lyric say?"

His amused expression caught her off guard. He seldom smiled unless Queen Vivant was around. "Stand up, Domi."

Ashamed for overreacting, she slowly stood.

"That's better. You'll have to ask your sister. I haven't spoken with her nor do I relay messages between females."

"I'll speak with her, My King."

He continued flipping the small trinket in the air. "I have no doubt you will. But duty first. Go to Jeru, then report for your shift early tomorrow. That's all I have for you."

She bowed again. She didn't realize she was almost running through the halls until she was out of the palace.

He won't punish me for ending that hateful wench! Thank The One!

She only hoped General Lyric would understand why she did it and forgive her. She could live without their mother, but she genuinely admired her older sister. She couldn't imagine being enemies with her.

T he warning chime of the TravelCraft started sounding loudly. She cursed.

"How could it run out of gas? I haven't been in the air for that long!"

She grabbed the controls, forcing it to lower over a large stretch of land. After what seemed like hours, she wiped sweat off her face.

"I've been walking for miles!" she muttered. "Just my luck to be stuck in the middle of nowhere with no signal to call for help!"

She gritted her teeth. "When I go home, I'm letting that transportation engineer have it! I don't care if he tells the king!"

That was a lie. She cared. A lot. About what the king thought of her and the preservation of her life. He was kind and fair, but he wasn't one to cross. Slapping away bugs off her arms, she knew she wouldn't be able to confront the engineer.

Getting on King Asa's bad side might prove to be a fatal consequence of being overly spirited. She wasn't ready to die. Not for a long time.

She spied a MaleForm on a horse coming down the hill too fast. Before she could move out of the way, the horse reared, sending her flying toward the ground. Angrily, she brushed grass and debris out of her hair.

"Why don't you watch where you're going?" she snapped.

The rider pulled on the reins, bringing the horse to a stop. "Me? Watch where I'm going? And who are you to give me orders?"

She peered into his gorgeous face, then at the magnificent horse.

His lip curled in what she perceived as sheer arrogance. "You have no idea where you are, do you?"

He looked vaguely familiar, yet she couldn't remember where she'd seen him before. Discourteous attitudes had always irritated her.

"No, I don't. Please enlighten me, oh great one!"

"I've always believed sarcasm sours a WomanForm's beauty."

She glared at him. "I couldn't care less about your beliefs. Just tell me where I am!"

His hollow laugh dripped with mockery.

"I've never been called great." He leaned forward on the saddle. "But in this realm, my title is *king*."

Her heart dropped in her chest as recognition washed over her. Sensing her discomfort heightened his amusement.

"Oh, you're getting it now, Miss Disrespectful? You must think highly of yourself to give orders to a royal. You're in my territory—Maieman. I belong here. How about you?"

His question threw her off guard. "I'm not sure. I've never belonged anywhere or to anyone."

The sincerity in her voice stirred his curiosity. He held the horse in place after it reared. "Proteus doesn't seem to like you very much. I can't say I blame him. What's your name, Miss I Belong To No One?"

Chapter 2

"I'm Domi," she said.

He snorted. "Sounds like a cheap pastry."

She held onto her patience. He was already hostile. Making him angrier wouldn't help her plight. "My name is Sergeant Dominia Cottes."

"Ah. You're in King Asa's army. I thought King Belial shot you in the back, not your head!"

She flinched.

"Maybe I'm mistaken," he said. "Maybe the blast rattled your brain if you think you can speak to me that way!"

"I apologize, Your Highness. I didn't recognize you."

"Then you should've asked before you let your mouth run like a broken dam! Trespassing on my territory and offending me is a record you alone hold. You can cool off your hot tongue in my confinement chamber until King Asa sends someone for you!"

"No!" she begged, getting on her knees. "Please don't do that!"

He moved the horse forward. "Why not? Are you too good for punishment?"

She swallowed. "I'm on good terms with my king, but I've seen what happens to Beings who rile him. If he finds out about this, he'll be furious with me."

Unmoved by her distress, he chuckled. "How is this my issue? You're trespassing on my land."

She pointed at her craft. "The TravelCraft ran out of fuel. I had no say in the matter!"

"Then you should've checked before you left Onzi! Again, none of this is my problem!"

Blaming herself for starting on the wrong foot with him, she thought of something to say that would ameliorate their acquaintanceship.

"King Jonah!" said Queen Marietta. "Don't be so harsh with her. She apologized. I've run out of fuel flying over the galaxy quite a bit in my day too."

"What does this have to do with this foul-mouthed heathen? Did you hear how she spoke to me?"

She surveyed the beautiful acres of flowers and shrubbery before refocusing on Domi kneeling on the ground.

"I did. And I heard her ask for mercy. She's no threat to us. Just a bit uncouth." The queen smiled at her. "You're General Lyric's sister, aren't you? I'm guessing you're hungry. Would you like to join us for luncheon?"

Impressed by the beautiful, silver-haired queen, Domi said, "Yes, Your Highness. To everything you've said."

Queen Marietta laughed when her son scowled at Domi. "Perfect! Climb aboard and hold on tight. By the time you freshen up, luncheon will be ready."

Shifting her eyes away from the furious king, Domi scrambled to climb onto the queen's horse.

Queen Marietta turned to the couple of soldiers who had followed her down the path. "Alert our transportation staff to bring our guest's craft closer to the palace and refill the tank. I want it to be ready once she's eaten and rested."

He saw the soldiers salute Queen Marietta, then glared at Domi. Without a backward glance, she started toward the palace with Domi's arms wrapped tightly around her waist.

Domi didn't dare look back at him—she wasn't a fool. The One had sent her a saving grace. She'd keep a tight rein on her shrewd tongue as long as she was in his presence.

T he queen led her into a bed chamber that was twice the size of the orphanage she'd grown up in.

"Here we are, my dear! You can bathe and change into clean clothes before luncheon." She opened the door to the largest walk-in closet Domi had ever seen.

"You're the size of my granddaughters. "There are rows of clothes they've never worn in here. You have your pick of what to wear."

Domi's breath caught in her throat. "Thank you, Your Majesty," she breathed.

"The bath chamber is filled with bathing salts, body oils, and just about anything else you could want. Luncheon will be ready in a half-hour's span. Don't be late." She winked at her. "King Jonah gets grumpy when he's hungry."

Domi wanted to slide to the floor. She selected something to wear and hurried into the bath chamber to bathe. Sinking into the rose-scented bubbles made her sigh with contentment.

"I was born for this!"

Since she'd joined Onzi's staff, Domi had become accustomed to eating delicious food. Yet, nothing had prepared her for the spread that graced King Jonah's table.

A steaming platter of fat duck breasts in a spicy and sweet orange glaze waited beside a large white crock of jasmine rice. She smiled gleefully at jumbo prawns and trout baked in lemon, butter, and thyme.

Another crock of potatoes whipped with heavy cream and butter sharply contrasted with the shimmering topaz tablecloth. More dishes delightfully flirted with her senses: a stuffed loin of pork, thick ribeye steaks, sautéed broccolini, stuffed mushrooms, and fresh ears of corn dripping with butter.

Dessert was a heavenly tart filled with orange curd and piled high with fresh whipped cream, a decadent cheese pie, and double chocolate gelato.

"Domi, I asked King Asa if it was all right for you to spend the night and go to Jeru in the morning," said Queen Marietta. "He said it was fine. After the day you've had, I think you'll accomplish your training much better after you've had some rest."

He snorted. "Soldiers have to be under conditions they don't like all the time. It comes with the territory. King Asa doesn't strike me as the type to coddle and pamper female soldiers."

"He isn't, and neither am I, son. Ensuring she receives a good night's rest isn't against the law. And I reared you to be respectful to guests. You're a king now. Being a proper host comes with the territory."

Domi wanted to laugh, but opted to focus on the delicious food. She suppressed a groan when she bit into a flaky cheese and chive biscuit. Not missing the mischievous gleam in her eyes, he glared at her while cutting into his steak. His knife sliced the meat so viciously, Domi believed he wished it were her neck.

"I miss them too, Jonah. But we must conduct ourselves the way Micah and Lucian would have wanted us to. We mustn't give up joy and hope. That's how creatures like Anemi win—if we give in to despair."

His irritated expression dissolved into placidity. "You're right, Mother. As always. I'll be a king my father will be proud of." He bit his lip. "And Lucian too."

Domi hadn't expected him to show vulnerability. Since she hadn't lost any of the family that mattered to her, she couldn't empathize with him. It wasn't her place to be informal with a royal, so she kept her mouth shut and focused on her meal.

She was a commoner. It was beyond gracious of the Krons to share their table with her. Taking note of the private dining chamber's expensive décor, she thought, *Next goal? Marry a king!*

Before the sun rose, he watched Domi's craft fly away from the palace.

Thank The One! She's gone.

"Jonah?"

He continued staring out the window long after the clouds hid the craft from his view.

"Jonah?" called Queen Marietta again.

When he didn't respond after the third time, she lightly tapped his elbow. "Jonah, this chamber isn't that large. Didn't you hear me calling you?"

Startled, he pivoted and looked into her eyes, trembling when she reached up and cupped his face.

"What's wrong, son? You look as if you've seen a ghost!"

A flash of pain ripped through his head, causing him to wince.

"I—uh—Mother?"

She grasped his shoulders. "What is it? Are you feeling ill?"

"I...I have a headache. I think I'll take some *Quozinite* and lie down. It's been a hectic day."

He stepped around her.

"I agree. How did the meeting go?"

Smiling falsely, he turned to her. "Oh, fine. Just the usual groaning and belly aching. Nothing for you to worry about."

She crossed her arms. "I heard the other kings want King Justin out of the way, but that's no surprise. That's his and Queen Revari's cross to bear. It's not our fight."

The pain throbbing in his head was overwhelming.

"You're right. I'm sorry, Mother. Please excuse me?"

"Of course." She brushed his hair off his forehead. "You've been working so hard. Go and get some rest."

He downed two *Quozinites* and dropped face-first into the mattress. Groaning, he pleaded for the pounding in his head to cease. King Micah's painting stared at him from a distance. If one didn't know better, they'd think the former king was weeping.

Queen Revari's past

Princess Revari entered Queen Opal's sitting room for the first time since she died. She shivered when the cool air hit her skin. Rubbing her arms, she wandered over to a beautiful crystal display of figurines in various shapes and sizes.

A WomanForm dressed in war armor caught her eye. Standing on her toes, she reached for it, catching the slim figure with her fingers. Concentrating hard, she pulled it to the front of the shelf. Just when she thought she had it, it slipped from her hands and shattered on the glistening platinum floor.

"What the hell is going on in here?!" thundered King Dubian. She shrank from his hostile glare.

"You! Who told you to come in here?"

"I-I was just—"

"Placing your dirty hands on things that don't belong to you! These belong to my Dellah! How dare you try and steal them!"

Roughly grabbing her by the collar, he dragged her into a supply closet behind the stables.

"Since you're so hell bent on destroying everything that means anything to me, make better use of your time here. Stand up on this bench."

When she did as he instructed, he grabbed two large buckets of horse manure and connected them to a long, steel beam.

"Squat down," he ordered.

He placed the beam behind her neck, forcing her to hold the heavy buckets.

"If your knees go to the bench or if you drop those buckets, your ass is mine. Do you understand me?"

"Yes, Father."

"Yes, King Dubian!" he roared. "Don't ever call me that! You don't belong to me! You belong to the devil!"

Her voice trembled. "Yes, King Dubian!"

His thin nostrils quivered. "The One took the wrong Being. It should've been you who died. Not my Dellah!"

She wanted to run from the madness in his eyes.

"He took her from me twice! What kind of Heavenly Father does that? Why did He punish me by leaving you here?"

Without another word, he whirled away, leaving the young princess helpless and alone.

"My King, the Queen of Maieman has arrived."

A box of chocolates lay before him on the desk. "What does she want?" he asked, greedily shoving them in his mouth.

Not bothering to wait for permission, Queen Marietta strolled in. "Your head. But I'll settle for seeing the princesses."

He stood to receive her. "Queen Marietta. What a lovely surprise!"

"Save it, King Dubian. Where are Princess Vivant and Princess Revari?"

"Well..." He nervously adjusted his collar. "Princess Vivant is a young WomanForm now. She goes as she pleases. She's on Jeru, visiting with friends. And Princess Revari is..."

"Yes? What about her?"

"She's ill."

"She was ill the last three times I came to visit her. I'm not leaving until I know she's all right. Where is she?"

"My Queen," said a Maieman soldier. "We've found the younger princess."

"**B**y The One! You evil monster!" she cried, rushing to relieve Princess Revari of the hefty buckets.

One of her soldiers stopped her. "Let me do it, My Queen!"

Once the princess was relieved of her burden, she pitched forward into the queen's arms.

"Dellah should've killed you when she had the chance!" screamed Queen Marietta. "If she were still alive, you'd be dead!"

King Dubian surveyed her calmly. "But she isn't." Pointing to Princess Revari, he said, "And there's the culprit!"

"Demented trash! You're filled with hate and ignorance! How dare you hurt this ChildForm?"

His empty, cold eyes swept over his daughter. "There isn't a scratch on her."

"And you'd better thank The One for that!" She cupped her face in her hands. "You're coming with me right now."

"That's not going to happen, Marietta. You do realize this is my realm?"

She whirled on him. "Is that so? Who is in charge of your military?"

Caught off guard, he trembled slightly.

"Ah! You catch on fast! Let me ask another question: Who is his mother? Better yet, do you think he'll stop me from taking her home with me? You have a handful of Platirian soldiers versus over fifteen thousand Maieman troops. If I were you, I wouldn't force my hand. I may not just stop with Princess Revari. I might ask my son to end you!"

He raised his hands. "Now, Queen Marietta, there's no need to cause such a ruckus over the ChildForm."

"She has a name. Princess Revari. That's what my friend named her before she died. I wish she'd never married you."

She nodded to a soldier. "Pick her up. We're returning to Maieman now." In midstep, she turned to King Dubian. "Don't even think about coming to retrieve her. You're no more a father than I am a bleating goat!"

"**P**rince Jonah, I brought a friend!"

He came running down the palace stairs. "Princess Revari!" he cried happily.

"Hi, Prince Jonah," she said shyly.

He danced around her long legs. "Mother! Is she staying with us now?"

"Of course. This is her home now."

"Marietta?" asked King Micah, coming out of the palace.

"She's not going back, Micah. And if he comes to claim her, I expect you to take his head. He's been torturing her while Gallium and Legend were away!"

"And what of her sister? I don't think they should be kept a part."

"Princess Vivant is almost a WomanForm now. She doesn't stay on Platirius. To avoid Dubian, she frequently visits other planets. I doubt she'd want to live here. She may visit with Revari, but I won't allow her to return with her to Platirius. Don't try and change my mind!"

He grinned at her. "Now when have I ever tried to do that, My Queen?"

The loving exchange between Prince Jonah's parents extinguished Princess Revari's loneliness. King Micah's twinkling hazel eyes were a stark contrast to her father's aloof, empty gaze. Until that moment, no MaleForm except Gallium had made her feel safe.

She couldn't imagine a life without King Dubian's verbally abusive tirades and scathing glares. She wondered if he'd allow her to stay with the Krons or would he drag her back to Platirius to endure more of his cruelty.

"I guess we have a daughter now, hm? He lowered to his haunches. "It's almost suppertime. What would you like to have?"

She seemed surprised by the question. "No one has asked me that since Aunt Opal died. She used to let me choose what I wanted to eat, but Father, I mean, King Dubian doesn't care."

He looked up at his wife. "Well, here we care very much. So what will it be?"

"Can we have steak? I like ribeyes."

He winked at her. "Princess Revari, I think you and I will get along just fine." Holding his hand out to her, he said, "Come with me and Prince Jonah. Let's make sure the dining staff cooks them just the way we like them, yes?"

For the first time since Queen Marietta rescued her, she smiled. "Thank you, King Micah!"

"I'll call Marcia Blight and place some orders with a couple of shops. She'll need a full wardrobe and lots of dolls and toys."

"Sounds as if you'll be busy with that. I'll have the ChildForms. You go have fun."

He kissed her and walked away with Prince Jonah and Princess Revari holding each of his hands.

Princess Revari lived with the Krons until she was well into her teen years. After she disappeared one night, Queen Marietta panicked.

"Micah! Have you seen Revari? I can't find her!"

Her thoughts raced together as she wrapped a fashionable tignon around her head. "He did it! He stole her just like he did with King Carlomon! We have to bring her back!"

King Micah shook his head. "Even if he did, we can't do that."

She stopped at the door. "Why not?"

"Lucian has a plan to take the throne. Now that the military is mostly comprised of our soldiers, he'll kill King Dubian and Chief Counselor Garoni. I've already selected a few of our justice counselors to add to his justice council. Revari will be safe under him and Vivant."

She sat next to him. "Thank The One. But what of Revari? I don't want her to think we've abandoned her!"

"We'll tell her everything when we go to King Dubian's DeathCeremony. If she wants to return with us, then it's fine with me."

"She'll come back," said the queen. "She will."

"You will marry Colonel Crisp. That is my order."

He leaned closer to meet her defiant eyes. "If you don't, I'll sever your head myself. But first, I'll start with your friend, Sergeant Legend."

A frantic Princess Revari found Gallium cleaning his weapons in the barracks.

"Gallium! Gallium, you have to help me!"

He put his sword down and reached for her. "Whoa, there! Slow down and take a breath!" He kneeled to her. "What's wrong?"

"He said he'll hurt Legend if I don't marry the colonel. He's old, Gallium. I don't want to marry him!"

"Your father?"

She nodded.

Rage flooded his handsome features. "Don't worry about the colonel or Legend. I'll take care of King Dubian."

She hugged him hard. "I love you. Please always remember that!"

"Why do you say that? What are you up to, Princess Revari?"

She held on to his neck and closed her eyes. "Nothing. Please don't worry about me."

He broke the embrace and placed his hands on her shoulders. "It's my job to worry. I'll always take care of you. Do you believe me?"

"Yes, but he sends you away to Earth. That's when he becomes unbearable."

His eyes hardened. "That's not going to happen anymore. I promised I'll handle him and I will! Go up to your bed chamber and stay out of sight until I come for you."

He threw Corporal Munt's body at the king's feet. King Dubian covered his nose from the stench of the decaying flesh.

"He got into some JunipBuds," announced Gallium. "I have no idea how that happened. You remember the JunipBuds, don't you, Your Highness?"

King Dubian looked to General Kron, but the general avoided his eyes.

"Princess Revari tells me you get insanely creative while I'm gone. If it's all right with you, I don't think Legend and I will be going to Earth on anymore assignments."

"Of course, General Barrios," said King Dubian. "Just...could you remove the body?"

Gallium shook his head. "No." He held out his hands. "You see, the poison is still on my hands."

King Dubian bolted from the throne just as General Kron started backing away when Gallium approached them.

"It's the strangest thing," said Gallium. "I think I consumed enough poison for a lot more bodies than this!"

"General Barrios," said General Kron. "We have no fight with you. There's no need to do this!"

"Yes, there is." He pointed to King Dubian. "He's not going to leave Princess Revari alone and I need to extract this poison from my system. It won't hurt me, but it would be a shame to let this beautiful venom go to waste."

General Kron thought quickly. "We have a few Platirian soldiers left. Use it on them."

King Dubian looked at General Kron as if he'd gone mad.

"Would you rather he sacrifice us, My King?" asked General Kron.

The king's shoulders drooped in defeat. "All right. Tell them I want them lined up outside the palace's gates."

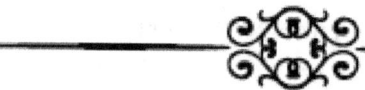

Over one hundred Platirian soldiers lay dead at Gallium's feet. Smiling at General Kron, he said, "We won't have any more misunderstandings where Princess Revari is concerned, right?"

General Kron stared at him before turning to his terrified soldiers. "Ship the bodies out of here immediately."

He left them standing with Gallium. Hearing him let out a string of curse words when he entered the den, Princess Vivant ran to him.

"What is it?" she asked. "What's happened?"

"Gallium just killed the last of the Platirian soldiers we had here."

Her mouth formed an O. "Why?"

He took her hand. "It was payback for your father threatening your sister."

Her breath hitched in her throat. "What did he do to her?"

"He ordered her to marry Colonel Crisp. He said if she didn't, there would be hell to pay."

"My sister isn't marrying that old bag! Colonel DeCosta is younger, stronger, and better looking. He'd be a perfect choice for her once she becomes the proper age!"

Her temper didn't rear its head often, but when it did, she reminded him of her mother. He hadn't fear her during her visits to Maieman, but shortly after he joined Platirius's army, he'd discovered 'Queen Dellah' was vastly different from the 'Aunt Dellah' he'd known all his life.

Not only had she ruled with an iron fist, she never hesitated in bringing it down on one's head. Or balls. Working under Queen Opal had been worse—her heart was as hard as a diamond. Grateful that Princess Vivant trusted him to handle things, he hastened to assure her that everything was under control.

"We don't have to worry about it now. Gallium made the king back off."

"Except for a few left on Kikhani, almost all our soldiers are Maieman." She looked up at him. "That's what you wanted, right?"

"Yes. Tell me where your head is. It's important to me."

He held his breath. If she was against the decision, it meant her father still had his claws in her.

"I think it's a good idea. It'll be easier to dethrone Father now." She held onto his hand. "I'm with you, Lucian. As long as you protect Revari and I, then I'm on your side."

A transmission was buzzing in on the queen's personal TeleScreen. Sleepily, she awakened to answer it.

Princess Vivant's tear-streaked face alarmed her.

"Princess Vivant? What's wrong?"

"It's Revari," she sobbed. "She's gone!"

"What do you mean she's gone? Where did she go?" She shook the king. "Micah? Micah, wake up!"

"What? What is it, Marietta?"

"She—she took a craft and left!"

"Could she be visiting friends on a neighboring planet? Calm down, darling. Everything will be all right!"

"Revari doesn't have any friends besides Jonah. Father never allowed her to have any!"

"Then where could she have gone?"

"I've tracked her to Earth!"

She almost dropped the TeleScreen. "Earth?! No! She doesn't know anything about that forsaken place!"

"I've been trying to reach her telepathically, but she keeps cutting off our sync! She doesn't want me to find her, Queen Marietta!"

"Honey, take some deep breaths. We'll find her! I promise. Where's Lucian?"

"I'm right here, Mother."

"You'll do everything in your power to find her, yes? She's so young, Lucian. The Humans will tear her apart if they learn what she is."

"She's a Platirian and that makes her superior to them. And our family. We'll find her, Mother. Don't worry."

"I'll send some soldiers to search for her too. Keep us informed, son," said King Micah. "Take Princess Vivant and have her lie down. It does no good for her to be so upset."

"Yes, Father. We love you both. In a while."

When they found Princess Revari, all hell broke loose. Anguish, despair, and betrayal threatened to disrupt the Kron family's close-knit bond.

"Y ou had her locked up in the Chamber of Despair?" cried Prince Jonah.

"No, Jonah. Her father did that. I just followed his orders. What else was I expected to do?"

"You could've called me to help her!"

"Are you insane, brother? I don't make the rules here!"

"You will when he dies! And that won't come soon enough! Platirian MaleForms are crazy! You have no idea what they'll do to her in there!"

"The last of the Platirian troops just flew in from Kikhani. I stationed them in the Chamber of Despair to keep them out of my hair. It's better that way," said General Kron.

"How could you be so stupid, Lucian?!" snapped Prince Jonah. "They torture and molest the WomenForm patients!"

"They won't lay a finger on Princess Revari. She's royalty. They're idiots but they're not suicidal. Princess Vivant will have their heads if they touch her sister."

"You've changed. How long have you been under his control? They'll wait for the right time to try and hurt her. You're just like him—you don't care what happens to Revari!"

General Kron shot up from the desk. "I'm nothing like him!"

"Then stop acting like it! Where is your compassion for other Beings?"

"I have none left for Platirians."

"Does that include Princess Vivant? Is she aware you don't protect WomenForms?"

The general's gray eyes narrowed. "Jonah, stay out of my relationship! I plan to marry Vivant. She's already stressed about Revari being locked up! I won't have you making things worse!"

"How can any of this madness get worse? Maybe I should talk to her and find out if she's aware you're doing nothing to stop the rapes and beatings that go on here!"

"Brother, I'm not the king!"

"You don't have to be!" snapped Prince Jonah. "You just need to have the heart of one!"

General Kron watched his younger brother storm off.

"You have no idea what it's like to deal with him, Jonah. For your sake, I hope you never do."

Chapter 3

In a rage, he marched into the Chamber of Despair. No one dared to deny the general's brother entrance. What he saw sickened him.

Beings were corralled in small spaces. Some were unclothed and severely underfed. Next to Princess Revari's chamber was a WomanForm who never stopped wailing. He peeked inside the glass shield. The princess lay motionless with her back toward the door.

The head NurseForm came to stand by his side.

"Is she...?" he asked.

"She's alive, but barely, Your Majesty. She consumes a few sips of water, but won't eat." She shook her head sadly. "I believe she wants to die."

He nodded toward the second door. "And what of her? Why won't she stop crying?"

"She's hungry. She bit the king the last time he was here. He's forbidden us from giving her food and drink."

"But she'll die!"

"He doesn't care, Your Highness. Every NurseForm here is committed to providing good care, but our hands are tied.

That new Platirian colonel will make our lives hell if we try to interfere! His soldiers—hurt the female patients."

She wrung her hands. "If we fight back, they'll hurt us too. They sliced up one of my NurseForms last week. She ended herself when she saw what they did to her face."

"What's his name?"

"Colonel Bracken. He's the last high-ranking Platirian soldier."

He smiled. *Perfect!*

"I'll take care of him. In the meantime, give her beef broth and applesauce. Once her body has adjusted, we'll move on to solid food."

H e found the colonel smiling at a pretty NurseForm who seemed less than impressed by his attention.

"Colonel Bracken! There's a disturbance down here!"

The colonel didn't hesitate to run after him. When they reached the hall, he looked around and said, "What are you going on about? There's nothing here!"

"Yes there is. Don't you see it?"

"See what?" he snapped impatiently.

"Death."

Prince Jonah broke his neck before he could blink. He nodded to a group of Maieman soldiers, hidden in a storage closet.

"Take him and the rest of the Platirian soldiers that came with him down to Coldarius's old border and execute them. Make sure my brother never finds the bodies. He'll think they abandoned their posts."

The soldiers saluted him. "Yes, Your Highness."

"Now things are about to change around here. For the better!"

P rince Jonah's personal rescue mission went into full effect. He teamed up with Dora Reese and Sandi Childler to maintain a regular meal schedule for the patients. No one went hungry anymore.

The laundry and cleaning staff got on board with cleaning and sanitizing every corner of the chamber from top to bottom. The beds were made with fresh, clean linens every week. Everyone was properly clothed when the seasons changed.

The prince ordered the decoration staff to paint the drab, pea green walls to baby blue and cream, and commissioned beautiful artwork to be hung on the walls. By the time he was done redecorating, the new platinum and cream marble floors shone like mirrors.

Treating the patients with dignity and respect made them happier. It gave them hope that they could return to their families and live outside of the chamber again. Thanks to him, many recovered and reentered society. But his victory was bittersweet. Princess Revari's condition had remained unchanged. He was determined to reach her.

S ix weeks later, she spoke to him.

"Leave."

"I will if you eat."

"You don't tell me what to do. You're a soldier."

To avoid startling her, he kept his face covered.

"So are you. Don't you remember?"

"Not anymore. I'd rather die than work under General Kron!"

"Dying isn't very fun, Princess."

Her beautiful silver eyes cut into him like daggers. "How would you know? You've never tried it."

"You're right. I haven't. But now that things are changing around here, more Beings are looking forward to life than death. We can keep that momentum going if you help us."

She took the bait. "What would I need to do?"

Q ueen Marietta entered King Dubian's meeting chamber and knocked everything off his desk in a single motion.

"You stole her from Micah and I! Now you have the gall to lock her away in the Chamber of Despair?!"

King Dubian calmly folded his puffy hands. His patronizing smile made her want to punch him in the throat.

"I only steal what's valuable. Revari is worth less than a Human."

He ducked when she threw a potted plant at his head. Sergeant Caper, not daring to glance in the queen's direction, focused on an imaginary spot on the floor.

"You're being unreasonable!" cried the king. "She broke one of our severest rules by copulating with a Human and bearing his spawn. Surely you don't think I'll allow the little whore to get away with it?"

His high-powered chair moved backward when she advanced toward him, fire flashing in her eyes.

"She's no whore! And it all can be laid at your feet! She went to Earth to be free of you!"

She pointed at him. "All of this is your fault! Not hers! She's not even twenty summers! Outside of Micah and I, she hasn't had anyone to teach her right from wrong! She wasn't aware consorting with Humans was illegal!"

For the first time, he realized General Kron had inherited her eye color—a sparkling, fiery gray. Her skin, akin to smooth caramel, looked soft and inviting. But not her eyes. He almost wilted under her glare. Almost.

"You haven't deceived me. You've kept her locked away to avoid accountability for what happened. But it's your fault.

Turning everyone against her to deflect from your failure as a FatherForm hasn't worked! What kind of Being are you?"

"I'm Platirius's king. That's all I need to be."

His haughty tone infuriated her. "Open that window," she commanded.

He sprang from his seat, his eyes wide with terror. "What are you doing? You don't take orders from her! I'm the ruler of this realm!"

"Not anymore," she said. "Throw him over the balcony!"

"Queen Marietta!" he shouted as the soldiers grabbed him.

They dragged him toward the window, ignoring his screams. The soldiers standing in the courtyard looked up when they heard the commotion. They started to enter the palace, but stopped when they saw the queen approach the window.

Immediately, they saluted her. She raised one hand to stop the soldiers from throwing him to his death and kneeled until she was at eye level with him.

"Now, my husband may hold compassion in high regard, but when it comes to you, mine goes out the window. Either you release Princess Revari from that dreadful place, or your brain will be splattered on that courtyard. Then? My son will rule Platirius. What will it be?"

"I'll do it! I'll release her today!"

She nodded her head. "That's a *good* dog, Dubian!"

S ighing with relief, he lifted his mask and breathed in the fresh air. Princess Revari would finally be released from the Chamber of Despair. He planned to find her and tell her how he felt about her. Then they could build a life together.

"Prince Jonah!" said King Dubian. "I knew something was up when Colonel Bracken and the rest of my soldiers disappeared. I never believed the AWOL story. It's been you all along! You told your MotherForm that Revari was locked up."

The prince's mocking laughter incensed him.

"Well, what can I say? You forced my hand when you wouldn't allow us to marry."

"This isn't Maieman, it's Platirius. I am in control here, not your mother!" He took a step toward him. "You'll learn what happens when I'm pushed too far!"

He laughed again and performed a mock salute when the king stormed off.

"Whatever you say, King Dubian!"

S till reeling with excitement about seeing Princess Revari again, he got into his craft. "Head for Maieman!"

"Yes, Prince Jonah!"

Suddenly, he felt sleepy.

"I'll close my eyes for a bit. When I'm home, Mother and I will arrange for Revari to be brought there."

H e woke up in the dark. Immediately, he sat up and squinted, his eyes searching the unfamiliar room.

"Look, troops. The pretty one is finally awake!"

He rose from a filthy, rusty bench. "Who the hell are you?"

"I'm King Joaquin, a friend of King Dubian's. You're in my realm now. Ziltach. The king has asked me to ensure you have a long stay with us in my confinement chamber. At first, I said no. Your brother isn't someone I want to tangle with, but he sweetened the deal."

His rotten, broken teeth were repulsive.

"Not only did he pay me, he promised me Princess Revari's hand. Make yourself comfortable. You won't be leaving anytime soon." He paused. "At least not alive. Beat him well."

His soldiers pounced on him, viciously pounding his head until he blacked out. As the years passed, the beatings became more frequent and severe.

They fed him moldy bread and beans for luncheon and supper. Breakfast was rancid porridge filled with maggots. He was given a single cup of water a day.

The toilet had been broken for years. He learned not to gag on the stench. He scratched at the worms that had laid eggs in his hair and beard. Sometimes he couldn't remember who he was or how he came to be in prison.

Occasionally, he awakened to the body of a dead soldier lying at his feet. After it happened for a third time, they'd stopped retrieving the bodies, leaving them to decay in front of him.

He learned to build fires and scrape the flesh off the bones. The Ziltachian soldiers were horrified when he polished the bones and made weapons.

King Joaquin had ordered him dead on several occasions, but the more soldiers he sent into the confinement chamber, the more he killed.

Soon, his cache of weapons was so astronomical, King Joaquin had no choice but to remove the new cadavers to prevent him from accumulating more.

Word of his success against the ruthless king had made its way around the work chambers. Intrigued by his strategic planning and bravery, some of the king's staff were willing to help him.

He paid a few in the processing chamber to smuggle in prime cuts of meat. Some sent heavy weights, while others provided fresh vegetables and fruit.

He put everything to good use. In time, his body transformed from lean to chiseled. The king had no idea his greedy staff's hatred of him fueled their desire to help his most minacious enemy.

One day, Prince Jonah was awakened by a massive explosion. The doors to the confinement chamber flew open.

His fellow inmates spilled out in droves, running toward the palace to kill the king. He followed them and was stopped by bright, blazing hues hovering over Ziltach. They were too late.

King Joaquin's severed head lay in the center of the courtyard. His body was suspended from a rope around his neck.

Beings were screaming and running away from soldiers clad in black armor while Ziltach slowly absorbed into a large black planet.

The unknown soldiers killed some of the prisoners. Their leader approached him, his onyx-covered BrainStaff illuminated from draining Ziltach's power.

"I'm King Asa. Ziltach is no more. I would've ordered your death too, but you look familiar. You're Prince Jonah, the lost son of King Micah and Queen Marietta, are you not?"

"Prince Jonah," he whispered. The name sounded unfamiliar to his ears. It had been a long time since anyone had called him that.

King Asa's sharp gaze assessed the scant, torn rags dangling from his body. "I think I'm right." He nodded to a couple of soldiers to take hold of him. "I doubt your family would want to see you in this state. Let's get you cleaned up before you return to Maieman."

"What is Maieman?" asked Prince Jonah.

The king looked at him sadly. "It's your home, Prince Jonah. Load him on a craft," he ordered.

The kingdom of Onzi was so large, it stretched across Space. It took six soldiers to hold him down to bathe and shave him. He screamed when the water hit his flesh, maggots and bugs dropped from his muscular frame.

The soldiers doused him with *Mecanite*, a strong-smelling powder made from lye and concentrated bleach, to kill any eggs that may have been left on his skin, before rinsing him off.

It was a struggle to dress him. He hadn't worn proper clothing in years. Now refreshed, his handsome face charmed the WomenForm dining staff until he growled at them like an animal. Terrified, they set a meal before him and fled.

King Asa watched him devour crocks of baked turkey wings, candied sweet potatoes, mashed potatoes, mustard greens, and a large pan of jalapeno and cheddar cornbread. He greedily licked the food from his fingers, grunting like a bear. Soon, he had emptied all of the dishes. His stomach growled.

"Still hungry?" asked King Asa, signaling for the dining staff to bring more food.

Prince Jonah ate everything placed in front of him and sat back, panting harshly.

"My doctors tell me your memory is shoddy. You've forgotten how to bathe, and your table manners are nonexistent."

Prince Jonah wiped his mouth with the back of his hand, scanning the table for any food he may have missed.

"I respect your father. It would kill him if he knew what you've endured. So, you'll stay here until you learn how to think and act like what you are—a royal." He leaned forward. "That's what you are—a royal MaleForm. Not the animal King Joaquin tried to turn you into. Do you understand?"

Prince Jonah pointed to his plate. "More meat."

After defeating King Hitam, General Kron was seated on a craft, headed out of Kikhani.

"Head for Maieman," he ordered. "I haven't seen my family in a long time."

Queen Marietta spotted him walking up to the palace. "Lucian? Lucian, you're alive!" she said, running to him with open arms. "I thought he'd killed both my sons!"

"Who?" asked General Kron.

"King Dubian! He lied about releasing Princess Revari! She's still locked up! And Jonah disappeared shortly before he dispatched you to Kikhani. He sent you away so you wouldn't find him. My baby has been gone for years!"

She shook his big shoulders. "King Dubian had a hand in it. Make him tell you where he is, Lucian!"

Realizing she was right, he held onto her, matching the fury in his father's eyes. Hoping to eliminate his claim to the throne, King Dubian had deliberately incited another war with the Kikhanians. He had no idea his brother had been missing.

"I will, Mother. No matter where Jonah is, I'll find him!"

"Now that the battle between Platirius and Kikhani is ending, I think General Kron will kill King Dubian," said Gallium. "He blames him for his brother's disappearance."

Princess Revari was on the floor doing push-ups. She was almost finished. "Ninety-eight, ninety-nine, one hundred!"

She jumped up and accepted the cool towel he handed to her. Wiping her face and neck, she said, "General Kron has been fighting on Kikhani for the past three years. He may have defeated King Hitam, but if he thinks he's going to be the next king of Platirius, I have news for him."

Gallium rolled his eyes. "So, he finally won against them? He was so arrogant, he thought the war would be over in a year."

"Yes, Platirius won, but they barely got out alive. Now that he's escaped death on Kikhani, I intend to introduce him to it once he's back on Platirius."

Rubbing his hands together, he asked, "You're going to kill General Kron?"

"I am," she said firmly. "He has it coming for what he did to my family."

"I'm all for you ending him. He'll return, walking around Platirius as if he owns it, bragging about how he's next in line to be king. He's disgusting."

"Disgusting...and soon to be stone-cold dead. I'm just getting started. And when I'm done, Platirius will never be the same."

He clapped his hands together once. "You'll need help. Sergeant Legend and I would be more than happy to assist you in getting rid of him. And King Dubian too. I feel bad for Queen Marietta. Now she and King Micah will never find out what happened to Prince Jonah."

"Who?" asked Princess Revari.

"My King and Queen! A craft has landed outside the gate!"

They looked at each other. "Lucian has arrived with Vivant and the princesses," said Queen Marietta excitedly. "I hope he has news about Jonah and Revari!"

Hand in hand, the king and queen ran out of the palace and down the path to the front gate. They stopped short when they saw who stood in front of them.

"King Asa?" asked King Micah. "This is a surprise. We're expecting Lucian and his family."

King Asa inclined his head to them. "I'm not sure where General Kron is, but I've brought someone who is eager to see you."

He stepped aside to reveal a striking, well-built MaleForm standing behind him.

"Hello, Mother and Father. It's wonderful to see you again," said Prince Jonah.

Queen Marietta screamed, running toward him. She and King Micah grabbed him, crying and shouting with joy.

"My son! My son has come home!" King Micah cried on his shoulder as the young prince held them in his strong arms.

Queen Marietta held his face in her hands. "Where have you been?" she cried. "We've looked everywhere for you!"

"I was imprisoned on Ziltach for years. King Dubian paid King Joaquin to capture me. He told me he sold Princess Revari to him too, but she wasn't there when King Asa took over. I know Lucian wants to be king, but I want Dubian's head first."

She peeked around his shoulder at King Asa. "You conquered Ziltach years ago. You mean you've had my son all this time?"

Prince Jonah placed a hand on his shoulder. "Mother, don't blame him. He helped me. I was in no condition to return to you the way I was."

"The way you were?" asked King Micah. "What do you mean?"

The prince's eyes hardened. "I was out of my mind. I had forgotten who I was and I...acted like an animal. Literally. King Asa taught me how to speak other than a few grunts mixed in with words, and how to eat with cutlery instead of my hands. I looked bad. And smelled bad. It would've brought you pain to see me that way. King Asa is my friend. We owe everything to him."

"It took that long to bring you back to sanity?" asked Queen Marietta.

"Yes, Mother. You have no idea what I endured on Ziltach."

"Thank you, King Asa. Thank you for bringing our son home," said King Micah.

King Asa nodded. "It was my pleasure."

"Yes, thank you, King Asa," said Queen Marietta. "My son is right. We're indebted to you now." She hugged Prince Jonah. "My baby is home! I can't imagine how much you've suffered!"

"Yes, and I'm glad to be free of it! And King Dubian is to blame. I want him dead. Where is he?"

The king and queen shared a glance. "Dubian is at a conference in another realm. Lucian is coming with Vivant and their babies. Please, Jonah, let it wait for a while. I know he'll want to see you!"

Prince Jonah nodded. "All right. When he gets here, we can put our heads together and take care of King Dubian for good!" He smiled down at his mother. "I don't think I can wait for them to eat."

She squeezed his arm. "We have plenty. And for you too, King Asa. Won't you stay with us for a while?"

He shook his head. "I should head back to Onzi."

Prince Jonah laughed. "He's tired of me. I'll bet he clicked his heels together when Maieman showed up on the radar!"

King Asa laughed. "It's not that. I've never liked imposing myself on others."

"You saved our son from a hellhole. Don't ever think you're intruding on us. I remember your mother. She was a very kind and decent queen. Just think of this as your second home, King Asa."

"When you put it that way, how can I refuse? Besides, he's been eating up my food for years. I'm long overdue to return the favor!"

A round of joyous laughter sounded in the air.

"Then let's go inside and feed you. There'll be plenty for Lucian when he arrives."

But General Kron never arrived that evening. Or the next. Prince Jonah was forced to resume his life not knowing when or if he'd see his brother again.

The present

"My Queen, King Jonah is back again."

Queen Revari was spread out on the floor, planting seeds in numerous, colorful pots. "For what?"

Sergeant Connie shook her head. "I have no idea, Your Highness. He said it's urgent."

The queen briefly closed her eyes and sighed. "Why do Beings bother me now that I'm trying to mind my business and live peacefully?"

She dropped a few rose seeds into the soil, covered them, and poured a bit of water into the pot. "There. That's the last of them. Place these on my balcony and tell Rynah I want them watered and fertilized every week! And dispatch the cleaning staff to tidy up in here."

"Yes, My Queen!"

She rose, brushing the bits of soil off her pants. "I'll go see what BongoHead wants."

H e was waiting for her among a row of enormous hydrangeas. He turned and smiled as she approached.

"It's such a pretty day. I thought we'd have an adventure!"

She looked from him to his craft.

"King Jonah? It's the middle of the day, and we both have realms to run. Surely, Maieman isn't that boring that you have time to plan leisurely activities whenever you want instead of working?"

"I *am* working. I'd like for you to return Maieman with me. I plan to visit some patients in my wellness chamber."

Her eyes narrowed. "You came here to ask me to go to a despair chamber?"

"We don't call them that anymore—"

She raised her hand. "I don't care what they're called now. I'm not stepping foot inside one of those things!"

"Revari, times have changed. They're not the torture chambers you remember!"

"You have one more time to drop my title so casually. I'm not one of your bed whores."

He raised his hands in surrender. "Forgive me. Queen Revari, may I have the pleasure of your company today?"

"No," she said flatly.

He sighed. "Many of the patients aren't comfortable having MaleForms enter their spaces, including me. I want to bring them comfort if I'm able to. I think seeing a beautiful queen would help tremendously."

Her sullen gaze provided the answer.

"Some of the patients are female ChildForms. The youngest is two summers."

Her expression softened a bit. "I've tried very hard to put my past behind me. I'm finally sleeping well at night. I don't wish to hurt my progress."

"Nor do I. But I think if you saw the work we're doing for my subjects, it would give you a better perspective on mental wellness."

She sighed. "You're not going to leave until I say yes, are you?"

She noted his beautiful teeth when his face split into a dazzling smile.

"No, and I'm considering throwing in luncheon if you accompany me."

She folded her arms. "I could always have my Revaltians drag you back to your craft."

He winked at her. "Now what have I done to deserve that? Besides, I'm on good terms with your soldiers. They have a reputation for being tough, but they're pretty nice ladies when you get to know them."

She stared at him for a moment. "I don't like my time being infringed on."

"I think spending time with those you care about is time well spent." He sighed and flexed his shoulders. "But what do I know? I'm just another ignorant MaleForm!"

"King Asa told you I called him that? I'm not surprised the two of you are friends."

He shrugged. "Why not? We're both young and successful. You'd learn he's a decent MaleForm if you'd give him a chance."

She clucked her tongue and shook her head. "I'll go to your realm today. But after this, don't return unless you're sent for. I've never given you the slightest invitation that I want to be friends."

"We're already friends. You just don't remember. But you will!" he said with an air of confidence. "Once you do, you'll see me in a better light."

"If you keep showing up unannounced, Queen Marietta will need a light too. To find your body up on the cliffs! You wait here."

He smiled at her. "Could I at least use a bath chamber? It's a long ride here, you know?"

Scowling, she turned to go into the palace. "The first door on the left at the end of the foyer. Be quick while I change."

"You already look stunning, but I wouldn't wear heels. We'll be doing a lot of walking after our ride."

He laughed again when the impudent look she tossed at him told him where he could go. In fifteen minutes, she was dressed in a dark burgundy suit. Her neck, wrists, and fingers were covered in diamonds.

A cute, round, saucy hat sat perched atop her long, natural curls. He fought the urge to kiss the full red lips that matched perfectly with her nails, and willed his member to be still when he caught a whiff of her spicy, seductive perfume. He couldn't despise her if his life depended on it.

He bowed at the waist to her. "I'll be the most envied MaleForm in my kingdom today."

"I thought we were going to visit ChildForms. I don't see where your ego fits into that."

Still bowing, he extended his arm to his craft. "After you, My Queen."

She approached the large craft and looked around. "This is a two-seater. Where are the passenger seats?"

"You're looking at it. You'll sit next to me."

"Are you insane? When I fly, I sit in the back. I hate heights!"

He leaned against the craft. "The formidable Queen Revari is afraid of heights? I don't believe that for a second."

"I didn't say I was afraid. I said I hated them."

"Then I'll have to make you feel so safe, whenever you're in a craft, you'll always think of me."

Giving her another wink, he opened the door and helped her into the craft. He caught her by surprise when he strapped her in as if she were a ChildForm.

"Safety first!" he said.

Having a front-row seat to flying over the galaxy wasn't something she was used to, but she reluctantly concluded the view was breathtaking. Hundreds of dazzling, colorful planets flashed before her eyes.

The galaxy's skies changing from day to evening was captivating and exciting to her. He witnessed joy flashing across her face and held back a smile.

You're almost where I want you to be, Revari. Almost...

Chapter 4

Far too soon, the ride was over. She stood by his side in front of a large structure with huge, opaque windows and high columns.

He warmed her cold hand in his. "The young ones will be so happy to see you. Some of them won't allow the NurseForms to comb their hair or read to them."

"Why would you have ChildForms locked in a wellness chamber?"

"A few lost their parents to illness and war. They have severe behavior problems—some of them have hurt the *FosterShip* parents we placed them with, so Mother and I have had a difficult time finding new families for them. Eventually, all of them go to good homes, but it isn't an easy task. It's not what you think. Let's go inside, and you'll see what I mean."

Queen Revari expected the smell of urine and feces to hit her nose when she entered Bêl, Maieman's largest wellness chamber.

To her surprise, the aroma of roses and lemons soothed her frayed nerves. The sharp click of her heels sounded crisp and clean as she strolled next to King Jonah, her small feet keeping up with his large, confident steps. If the NurseForms were surprised by her visit, they kept it hidden under their warm, inviting smiles.

"Ah, NurseForm Jax! It's nice to see you again," said King Jonah.

NurseForm Jax had a round face and kind eyes. Her heavy locs were coiled into a neat ball on top of her head. She and all the NurseForms bowed to the royal figures.

"It's wonderful to see you again too, Your Majesty!" Turning to Queen Revari, she said, "Her Majesty has blessed us with her presence today. The ChildForms will be so happy to see you."

"It's a bit before luncheon time, isn't it? I was hoping to drop off some toys and candy before the dining staff begins serving them."

NurseForm Jax clapped her hands in delight. "That would lift their spirits! We cannot thank you enough, Your Highness."

He smiled down at her as a robotic cart filled with toys, books, and candy rolled toward him.

"This looks amazing! We'll get on our way then. I'll see you later, NurseForm Jax!"

She nodded and bowed. "Have fun, Your Majesties."

Queen Revari inclined her head toward the NurseForms, yet kept silent. Despite the beautiful furnishings and designer art hanging from the walls, she still felt uneasy.

Focusing on the vast display of dolls on the cart saddened her. While Queen Opal had lavished her with beautiful possessions, after she died, her father had confiscated and burned them.

Once Princess Vivant turned eighteen summers, she tried to resume her sister's LifeCelebrations out of defiance for their father's cruelty. After he tossed a six-layer cake across the ballroom, she gave up.

Every year, until she ran away to Earth, she'd had lavish gatherings with her sister, King Micah, Queen Marietta, Prince Lucian, and... Stopping abruptly at the memory, she wildly searched his face. The cart stopped moving when they did.

"What? What's wrong?"

"You," she said and clamped her mouth shut. "I spent some of my LifeCelebrations at your palace!"

His handsome face broke into a grin. "See? I knew coming here would jog your memory!"

She shook her head. She didn't want to remember. She had convinced herself that whenever she was happy, it would end in despair. "This wasn't a good idea. I'd like to leave."

A petite female ChildForm peeked around the corner. Her unruly, sandy-brown curls were in desperate need of grooming.

"Hi, King Jonah!" She pointed to the cart. "Are those for us?"

Smiling at Queen Revari, she asked, "Is she your wife, Your Highness?"

The king's smile widened. "Not yet, but time will tell, Basna!"

The queen thought she'd die of embarrassment when he winked at her. Basna's face took on a delightful glow.

"She's beautiful!"

"Yes, she is. Choose anything you like."

After she'd selected a doll and a book, he said, "Shall we go and give these to your friends?"

"Yay! Let us go!" said Basna.

Queen Revari hid a smile when he said, "After you, My Queen."

For nearly an hour, they made deliveries to the youngest members of Bêl. Queen Revari marveled at how many were displaced after losing their ParentForms in wars.

The ChildForms smiled, waved, and gave her high-fives, making her feel welcome in their little world.

She was pleased to see their personal quarters were beautifully furnished. Clean, fresh sheets and fluffy comforters decorated the beds.

Dozens of toys, sturdy bookcases filled with books, and tiny furnishings complemented the roomy spaces. Subtle notes of jasmine and lavender rose from the soft, thick carpets.

Bêl didn't look like anything she'd ever experienced. She hadn't built any mental health chambers on Revani, yet after seeing the remarkable work of the staff, she was inspired to follow his lead instead of sending her Beings to Platirius and JanIus for mental wellness care.

The small patients were groomed and well-nourished. When the chime for luncheon sounded, they dutifully went to their bath chambers to wash their hands before following each other down the long corridor to a large dining chamber. In a single file, they collected utensils and extended their plates to the dining staff.

The king sniffed the air. "Venison roasts are on the menu today. Do you like venison, Queen Revari?"

"Yes, I do. Will we eat with the ChildForms?"

She wondered if he knew how he looked at her made her feel like a TeenForm again.

"I usually do when I visit, but if you don't want to, we can go up to the palace and dine with Mother."

"No," she said quickly. "Here is fine."

His eyes twinkled at her. "You don't want to see Mother?"

"I doubt she'll want to see me," she said dryly. "I'd rather not have my appetite spoiled. I don't mind eating with the ChildForms. I've never had the opportunity to do it before now."

He selected two plates and added utensils and linen napkins. "She's not angry with you anymore. Neither am I. After a while, we both agreed King Anemi would've killed Lucian even if you hadn't drugged him on his craft."

He sighed. "No one, including me, could escape your father's insanity. I can only imagine how terrible it was for you to live with him all those years."

She took a plate from his hands. "What did he do to you?"

A dark look clouded his face. "I don't want to talk about it. I'm having a great time with you and the little ones. Let's not ruin it by discussing him."

Although curiosity was killing her, she didn't push for an answer. If he wanted to share parts of his past with her, he'd do it in his own time. The dining staff added generous portions of venison, stewed chicken, mashed potatoes, fried corn, and candied sweet potatoes to her plate.

A smile peeked out when one of them brought slices of peach pie à la mode to their table. "Peach is my favorite pie!"

He winked at her. "I'm aware. I asked my royal baker to bake a couple. I know all of your favorites."

The ChildForms asked her a bunch of questions that she tried to answer honestly. They wanted to know if she had sons or daughters their ages, who did her hair, where she got her clothes, and if there were ChildForms in her realm. She found she enjoyed their company.

You enjoy spending time with Jonah too, she thought.

By the time luncheon ended and her tiny hosts had cleared outside to play, she was touched by their acceptance of her. There was one doll left on the cart. It was dressed in an elegant, flowing topaz gown. Her long, black hair and brown skin were the perfect complement to her clothing and jewelry.

"We forgot one," she said.

"No we didn't," he said, taking the doll off the cart. "This one belongs to you."

73

She couldn't hide her surprise when she reached for it. "There are dozens more just like it at my palace."

Startled, she looked up at him. "So...you have a young daughter?"

She hated admitting to herself that she loved the way his laugh made her feel. As if she'd just stepped out of a warm bath.

His warm hazel eyes sparkled at her. "No, but maybe someday I'll find an amazing WomanForm to help me with that."

"Then why do you have them? I doubt Queen Marietta collects them."

"She did once. For you."

She traced a finger down the doll's satin dress. "What are you talking about?"

Hearing the happy ChildForms playing ball on the field reminded him of the time they'd spent together.

"When we were their ages, you lived with us. Mother brought you home after she visited Platirius one morning. She said she'd had enough of your ignorant father's ways and wouldn't stand for it anymore."

"Did Vivant come?"

"No. He wouldn't allow her to leave. But we grew up together."

Her mind drew a blank when she tried to remember. "Happiness hasn't always come easy to me or stayed with me for long. How could I forget an entire period of my life?"

Moving a lock of hair from her face, he said, "I think losing your family did quite a number on you. Being locked away in that hellhole did you no favors. By the time I found you, you were so far gone, you wouldn't eat or sleep. It took some time, but eventually things got better and you had a job."

He tapped the doll. "Like this. It was your responsibility to deliver books, flowers, whatever made Beings happy. You made deliveries every week until you were discharged. When Mother forced his hand, he promised to let you go, but he lied. Thank The One, after I...left...the NurseForms continued treating the patients humanely. By then, all the soldiers were Maieman, so they remained loyal to my family, not him."

She couldn't imagine Queen Marietta challenging her father.

"Why would she care if I rotted in there or not?"

His kind eyes looked deeply into hers. "My mother and your mother were best friends. Queen Dellah visited her the night before you were born. Mother said she almost made her stay, but she knew she had to return to Platirius. I think she was planning to have your father executed, but she died."

It was too much for her to take in. The Krons had been her SecondFamily? Had she forced herself to wipe out all the memories she had after she and Oliver were kidnapped and brought to Platirius?

Perhaps she couldn't bear to hold on to anything except the family she'd lost—her husband and baby. Repaying her father, General Kron, and her sister had kept her going for many years. For the first time, she realized how much she'd lost.

They reached the end of the dining chamber where five baskets of blue lemons, mangos, strawberries, dates, mint chocolates, caramels, and other tantalizing treats sat waiting on a counter.

"Who are these for?"

He added the baskets to the cart trailing behind them. "One is for you and the others are for Vivant and my nieces. I'm paying them a visit this evening. Would you like to join me?"

"No, I've already seen Vivant. After I leave here, I'm flying to JanIus to spend the night at my son's palace. I want to see him and Fawn."

"Dr. Azini?"

"Yes, do you know her?"

"I met her briefly when we took down King Anemi. She seems like a nice WomanForm."

"Well, you keep your eyes off her. She and my son are an item now."

A large red craft flew over the palace and landed in front of Bêl.

He grinned at her. "Looks like the cavalry has come for their leader. The doctor is safe from me. My eyes are reserved for the most beautiful queen in the galaxy. Shall we go?"

He walked her to her craft where General Legend and Colonel Sheila were waiting.

"I had a really good time, Your Highness. Thank you for making the ChildForms so happy."

Taking the largest fruit basket, she said, "You're welcome. I enjoyed myself too."

Eagerness lighted up his face. "Does that mean you'll visit again?"

"Maybe. I never make promises I don't keep."

"How about one? Promise you won't forget me?"

She looked at him and said, "I don't think you'll have to worry about that. In a while, King Jonah."

Had she been the melting type, she would've been a puddle at his feet. Instead, she kept her back straight and her face free of emotion. She wasn't comfortable with how happy he made her, nor did she feel the need to share it with him.

Yet, he smiled as if he *knew* how his presence twisted her inside out. That put her on notice. King Jonah wasn't the mousy, meek, goody-goody she thought he was. He was a very masculine, primal, strong-minded MaleForm who knew exactly what he wanted. Her.

"In a while, My Queen."

Colonel Kourtney approached Queen Vivant. "My Queen, you have a visitor! King Jonah is here to see you."

"Surprise!" he said. "I hope I'm not disturbing you." He held up the gift baskets. "I promised the princesses I'd bring them some blue lemons after they ripened."

"Jonah!" said the queen, hugging him. "You know you don't need an excuse to visit!" She took a basket. "These lemons smell glorious! The princesses will be so happy to see you! Why don't you stay for the night? I'm going to Onzi."

"Oh, is it the weekend already?"

She blushed when he winked at her.

"Yes, it is," said King Asa, coming up behind him. "And I'm here to take my lady back with me." He bowed to Queen Vivant, kissing her on the hand.

Princess Tarah came running down the stairs. "Mother! Tyre won't return my hairclips! Uncle Jonah! You're here!"

Laughing, he picked her up and swung her around. "Of course! I brought your lemons as I promised."

"Uncle Jonah!" cried Princess Teenah and Tyre.

He hugged each of them and stood back to look at them. "You're as beautiful as your mother, but I see Lucian in you too. He'd be so proud of you if he were here."

Each princess took a basket of lemons. "Ooh, look at these! I want to make blue lemonade!" said Princess Teenah.

"Let's bake lemon and blueberry scones too!" said Princess Tyre. "Can you imagine how good they'll look? We'll have to post them on our social media pages! Only Maieman has blue lemons. Everyone will be so jealous!"

"Princesses," said Queen Vivant. "Mind your manners and thank your uncle for thinking of you."

"Oh, thank you, Uncle Jonah!" they said.

Princess Tarah noticed King Asa and nudged her sisters. "Hello, King Asa."

Each of the princesses bowed to him.

"Mother is going on another date!" said Princess Teenah.

Suddenly, thunder and lightning ripped through the sky as a heavy wind picked up. Heavy rain shot down on them hard and fast.

"What on Platirius?" asked Queen Vivant. "How could a storm be coming now?"

Before anyone could answer, a bolt of lightning hit King Asa's craft, shattering the glass.

"My King," called an Onzian soldier. "The engine is damaged!"

"Ours too, King Jonah," said a Maieman soldier.

"All right, clear out and join the queen's soldiers in the barracks. We can't leave until the crafts are repaired," said King Asa. He eyed the incoming tornado headed fast for the palace. "We won't be going anywhere any time tonight. Let's go inside!"

The queen dispatched a call to Major Sonee. "Activate the protective shield around the palace. I'm staying here tonight!"

"Yes, My Queen!"

She turned to King Asa. "It looks like I'll be entertaining you at my home this weekend. Is that alright with you?"

"You know it is," he said, giving her a seductive wink. "This will be an interesting weekend, don't you think?"

Her eyes glowed with anticipation. "Stormy nights make the steamiest nights!"

H e stood naked in front of a roaring fire, his arms and legs shaven clean of hair. Chanting an old spell, he dropped bits of bloodied cloth and a lock of hair into a pot simmering over the fire.

Closing his eyes, he murmured a string of mysterious utterings, willing the shadows to uncover what he wanted to see.

Straining his eyes into the distance, he realized the spell had satisfied his insatiate curiosity to see them for himself. *There they were!* Over a dozen spirits of fallen Platirius kings roamed the grounds.

Dark circles sat under black eyes burning with rage. Their once splendid robes and cloaks were torn and dirty, hanging in ribbons of rags around their mottled flesh.

"Vengeance!" they chanted over and over. "Death to King Justin!"

Aggrieved and forgotten, their souls had been left to wander aimlessly, seeking retribution for past transgressions. He smiled. Knowing his plan was succeeding made him feel warm inside. Soon, King Justin would be in for a surprise. One he'd never forget.

K ing Asa quietly slipped his nude form beside a sleeping Queen Vivant. He wrapped his arms around her when she called his name.

"Asa?"

"Shhh, everything is all right now. The storm is passing. Sleep, my love."

She turned and settled into his arms as he looked up into the stars—tiny chips of light in a sea of overwhelming darkness.

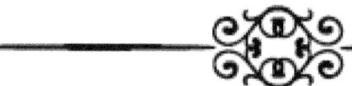

Queen Revari rubbed perfumed cream over her body before slipping into a gold, satin night robe and pulling the covers up to her chin. She usually loved reading a good book before bed, but the day's events had her mind too discombobulated to concentrate.

Why don't I remember living at King Jonah's palace with his family?

Frustrated, she turned over and punched her pillow. It was going to be a long night.

A dark figure chased King Jonah through waist-length grass. No matter how much he increased his speed, it didn't widen the distance between them.

The faster they ran, he could feel the shadow catching up to him. His heart pounding in his chest, he struggled to breathe.

Suddenly, he spied a cliff in front of him. He tried to slow his pace, but it was too late. He screamed when he dived headfirst into the darkness.

"Teenah, please pass the scrambled eggs?" asked King Jonah.

"Plain or the ones with cheese and jalapeño?"

He grinned at her. "What do you think, niece?"

"Cheese and jalapeño it is!"

"Thank you!"

He helped himself to a hefty scoop of the eggs and placed them beside a mound of fried potatoes and bacon.

Queen Vivant slathered butter on a blueberry muffin and bit into it. "That was some storm last night!"

"Yes, it came out of nowhere, but I'm glad the transportation staff were able to repair the crafts," said King Asa.

Princess Tarah looked up from her plate, observing him. "It's nice to have Mother here on a weekend."

Ignoring Princess Tyre's gentle kick from under the table, she concentrated on adding brown sugar and apples to her porridge.

King Asa picked up on the subtle slight.

"I'm looking forward to exploring more of the grounds. I seldom have time to take breaks from my realm, but I'm enjoying my visit."

King Jonah lifted his glass. "I'll drink to that!"

"Jonah, you should bring Mother next time. I worry about her being left alone now that Father is gone."

He laughed. "Why? She's as young and spry as she was when we were ChildForms. She keeps busy with the ChildForms we're trying to find homes for, and she's a competent leader. I think I learned how to rule more from her than Father—he was the easygoing one. Mother is a lioness."

"I agree, but even lionesses become lonely. I want her to know we're here for her. Maybe she should come here to live with us now that you're king? I'm sure you'll want to settle down and raise a family of your own soon."

He took a swig of orange juice. "I'm in no rush. When the right WomanForm finds me, I'll be ready. I think I'd be very depressed if I didn't live with Mother."

King Asa glanced at him before reaching for more waffles.

"Yes," whispered King Jonah. "I'd be overwhelmed indeed."

"Did you say something, Uncle Jonah?" asked Princess Tarah.

"Oh, nothing! I'm just thinking of all the things I need to do when I return to Maieman."

The princesses sought each other's gazes and bit their lips to keep from smiling. They started eating again when their mother raised her brow.

Noticing something was amiss, he said, "Is there something I should know about?"

"No," said Queen Vivant. "You should try the peach jam. Dora Reese made it last night. It's heavenly."

Intrigued, he picked up the small pot of jam. "Dora's food is legendary. It still tastes just as good as I remember when I was a ChildForm. You know, I know a Being who would appreciate a couple of jars of this."

She smiled at him. "I already packed a big basket with peach syrup, a couple of peach pies, and more of Dora's creations. Would you mind giving it to her?"

"No, not at all," he said. "I'll drop by Revani before I head home this evening."

There's something else I wouldn't mind giving to her.

"Don't go until after supper. Pork with peach applesauce is on the menu. Dora stewed some of the peaches we harvested." She closed her eyes in delight. "I can't wait to taste it!"

"Me either. All right, it's a deal! I'm staying for supper."

The beautiful weather turned the fierce storm that had raged over the queendom into a distant memory. The kings played ball games with the queen and the princesses, swam in deep ponds, and smoked chicken, brisket, and beef sausages in the shade.

Sandi Childler brought large bowls of potato and macaroni salads from the dining chamber and placed them aside bowls of broccoli salad and fruit salad, a large dish of blueberry cobbler, and round pitchers of sweet tea and lemonade mixed together.

King Jonah laughed when Princess Tyre pushed Princess Tarah into a pond. She popped up like a jack-in-the-box, sputtering and muttering curses under her breath.

"Who knew Platirius could be so peaceful?" he said.

"It's what you make of it," said Queen Vivant. "It would've been this way if Father hadn't been deranged."

"I think you've done a fine job of leading it," said King Asa. "Everyone looks so happy."

"I make rounds the way Mother used to before she passed," she said. "I don't want anyone to suffer the way we did when he was alive. Revari doesn't think so, but I believe Platirius can rise above its toxic past. If spirits walk the grounds, the only one I've seen is King Anemi. I think it's just silly talk to keep Beings afraid."

King Jonah and King Asa shared a look.

"Rumors and rubbish complement each other. Let's not spoil this beautiful day discussing things that can't hurt us."

"I agree." She lifted her drink. "To new beginnings."

As the royals clinked their glasses, King Dimaro's evil spirit smiled.

"Hello, Vivant! Is Jonah headed back?"

"Yes, Mother, he just left. But he's making a detour. I asked him to take a basket of sweets to Revari."

"I see," said Queen Marietta. "They've been spending a lot of time together, but she hasn't come to the palace."

"Give her time, Mother. It's hard for her to let Beings inside her heart."

"I hold no ill will toward Revari. I looked at her as a daughter once."

"That was before she sent Lucian out on that bogus mission and he never returned. I've forgiven her, Mother, but have you? In your heart?"

Queen Marietta looked out a window and sighed. "Your mother and I were good friends since we were ToddlerForms. Seeing her again made me realize how much I've missed her. And she was right. There's been far too much bitterness and fighting between our families. It's time for it to end. Long past time."

Queen Vivant smiled. "Does that mean Revari is invited to Jonah's surprise LifeCelebration tomorrow?"

"Of course. I don't think he'd have it any other way."

Queen Vivant bit her lip in anticipation. "Do you think they're getting closer?"

Noting the note of hope in the younger queen's tone, Queen Marietta said, "I think Jonah wants it, but I'm not sure about Revari. I suspect she's still in love with that Human."

"Well, if anyone can take her mind off him, it would be Jonah. She hasn't come close to receiving love since he died. It's time she let go of the past and embraced the future. I would be ecstatic if she and Jonah became an item. They're perfect for each other."

"If I had fought your father when he stole her from me, maybe she wouldn't have gone to Earth. She and Jonah would be married by now."

"You shouldn't blame yourself for the past. There's still time for them to be together. They're destined for each other."

"You and I know it, but what about her son? Would he be willing to accept her forgetting about his father? Siring him with a Human is a mistake she's still paying for."

"It's not up to Justin. Revari is a grown WomanForm who makes her own rules. He has no say in who should make her happy and who shouldn't."

"I agree, Vivant. I expect you and my granddaughters to be here at six tomorrow evening. I can't wait for you to see the cake. Our dining staff's skills are unsurpassed!"

"If it's chocolate, Tyre will be chomping at the bit for a piece."

Queen Marietta laughed. "Give my love to them. I'll see you tomorrow. Oh! The theme is our signature color: topaz! And don't forget to wear the masks I sent you!"

"Yes, Mother. We'll be there. In a while."

"In a while, Vivant. I love you."

Chapter 5

Queen Revari frowned when Marcia Blight held a svelte topaz dress under her chin.

"Are you happy with it, Your Highness?"

"It's beautiful, but I'm having second thoughts about going to the LifeCelebration. I've never attended any events on Maieman. Why start now?"

"Because King Jonah would be crushed if you didn't go," said General Legend.

"He doesn't know it's happening, Legend. Even if he did, I doubt he'd miss my presence."

General Legend examined her manicure. "Now, you know that's not true, Your Majesty. Anyone can see he's smitten with you."

"Or he's seeking revenge for his brother," muttered the queen.

"My Queen, you must learn to trust others. If Gallium and I thought for one second King Jonah was trying to hurt you, we'd end him. We all know who really killed General Kron. I don't think he's holding it against you. Otherwise, he wouldn't have allowed you to visit the ChildForms at Bêl. You've been very successful in helping him find homes for all of them. I think that meant a lot to him."

"I love ChildForms. Everyone knows that. As for trust...I give it when it's earned."

"And if he never does anything you deem worthy of trust? What happens then?"

She shrugged. "Nothing. I don't feel anything for him, so I won't be offended."

The general tossed her an impish smile.

"What? I don't! Nothing about him moves me—not his eyes or his smile, or his...dimples in his cheeks!"

Her smile became wider. "In which cheeks?"

"Oh, stop it, Legend! You're looking for things that aren't there. Thank you, Marcia. I'll take the gown."

"It's my pleasure, Your Majesty."

After she bowed to her and held up her palm, the queen transmitted the cost of the gown and a generous bonus.

"General Legend, I sent over your gown and General Barrios's suit by night mail. I received confirmation they were delivered."

"Yes, I got them and they're perfect! Thank you so much, Marcia. I can't wait to see my husband dressed up again!"

She raised her palm to receive the second payment and bowed. "Thank you both. Please call me anytime."

"She does incredible work," said Queen Revari, still observing the gown.

"Yes, she does. I can't wait to see the look on King Jonah's face when he sees you!"

"And why is that?"

They both turned to see King Justin standing in the doorway.

"Justin! When did you arrive?" asked Queen Revari.

He gave her a quick peck on the cheek. "Just in time to hear Aunt Legend going on about you and King Jonah. What *is* going on with you two?"

Queen Revari patted his arm while a Revaltian took her gown and hung it in her enormous walk-in closet.

"Nothing for you to worry about. Daria, place the shoes below the gown."

"Yes, Your Majesty."

"Normally, I wouldn't worry, but after what happened with Beeman, it's hard for me to trust strangers."

"Jonah isn't a stranger," said General Legend. "He and your mother have known each other since they were ChildForms. They were good friends."

"So, what happened?" he asked.

"That was before I met your father. I forgot him along with most of the memories I had when I lived in the galaxy."

"I've read depression does that to you," said King Justin.

"If he'd really meant anything to me, I wouldn't have forgotten."

"That's not true, My Queen. Before Queen Dellah restored your memories of Coldarius, you'd forgotten a lot of memories about Gallium and me too."

King Justin was grateful for his aunt. She was one of the few who was allowed to be open and honest with his mother without her flying off the handle.

The queen sighed and sat down. "I guess you're right. I promised Mother I'd make a fresh start with my life and I intend to. But there's no room for love in my life. I'm content with how things are. I'll never marry again."

"Stop saying that," admonished General Legend. "You don't know what The One has in store for your life. Love isn't something we're blessed with once and that's it. Please don't close your heart off to what could be."

"I think Mom is right. You say they were friends, but that was a long time ago. She knows next to nothing about him now. What if he's just as ruthless as his brother was?"

"Would a ruthless king bring an injured General Lyric to the institute?" asked General Legend. "If he were heartless, he would've left her in the Averlands. He was under no obligation to help her, but he did."

She got up and started placing small, crystal bottles of bath salts and oils into a basket for the queen to bathe.

"He and Queen Marietta helped us defeat King Anemi *and* the general's clone. It couldn't have been easy for them to learn he was gone for good after hoping he was alive. I think he deserves more credit than you're giving."

King Justin lowered his head for a moment, thinking. "You have a point, but I'm not letting my guard down just yet. She's my mother. I have a responsibility to protect her."

"No, that responsibility belongs to me and the Revaltians under my command. You have a kingdom to look after. Start there."

"She's my mother," he protested. "She's—"

"Lived for more years than you can count. Millions. She's a headstrong WomanForm who is always in control of any situation she faces. Treating her like an innocent ChildForm is a bit much, don't you think?"

His nostrils flared. "I understand WomenForms—especially her—can take care of themselves! But MaleForms aren't thorns you weed out when it's convenient. I intend to make sure this King Jonah doesn't hurt her. I respect you, Aunt Legend, but you won't stop me from protecting her!" Inclining his head to the queen, he said, "I'll see myself out!"

General Legend sucked her teeth. "Ugh, that awful male pride! What happened to our easy-going, accommodating young Justin?"

Queen Revari smiled. "He's growing up. And he has my temper. I sense he's a bit miffed about his father. It's sweet irony. He told me I should be more open to love."

They stared at him as he angrily marched to his craft.

General Legend closed the shutters. "He said that?"

"I think he's afraid I'll forget about Oliver, but that'll never happen. Falling in love with him was one of the best experiences of my life. Nothing will ever replace the time I spent with him."

After the craft took off, General Legend said, "Well, I agree with him about one thing: it is high time you let love have a place in your life. His feelings might be hurt, but he'll get over it. He didn't like it when you interfered in his and Lyric's relationship. I intend to remind him of that if he tries to do the same with you and King Jonah."

"I don't think you'll need to. As I said, there's nothing going on between the king and I."

The general nodded her head toward the basket filled with baked goods. "Oh no? What does that tell you?"

The queen sighed and grabbed a bathing cloth. "It means my sister and Dora Reese were thinking of me, nothing more."

"Ah, but they sent King Jonah to make a special delivery when they could have chosen one of the Vivacians."

Queen Revari softly flicked the bathing cloth in her direction. "You're reading too much into things, sister. I'm off to bathe. Have Kia send up some mint chocolates and PotterBerry wine."

General Legend picked up a jar of peach jam and smiled. "As you wish, Your Highness!"

"Uh oh," said Fawn. "You don't look happy. Did something happen with General Lyric, My King?"

King Justin glanced at her before shaking his head. "First, I haven't seen Lyric since the accident. Second, I thought you and I were getting closer. Why are you asking about her?"

She shrugged. "She was your first love..."

"In space," he said. "She isn't the first one I've had."

He moved closer and placed his hands on her shoulders. "Listen, I don't want you to worry. Nothing is going to be rekindled between Lyric and I. Her mother was a very cold dash of water in my face. I realized I was putting myself last in our relationship. I don't intend to make the same mistake twice."

"I see. If it isn't love, then what's bothering you, Your Highness?"

He sighed. "I wish you'd stop calling me that in private."

She shook her head. "Sorry, I can't."

He cocked his head. "How about after we're married? What will you call me?"

Her golden brown eyes sent his libido over the edge. "I don't know. I haven't been proposed to."

"Ah! That's because you've been too busy at the institute to let me!"

"I have some free time coming soon," she teased. "Now, may I please know what's bothering you?"

He groaned. "It's my mother."

"I thought you two were getting along."

"We are, but... There's this king who's sniffing after her like a mutt in heat. I know it sounds crazy, but it's getting on my nerves! I mean, I know I told her she should find love, but now that it might be happening—"

"You're not on board with it," she finished. "Is he mean to her?"

He scoffed. "If he were, he'd be dead. You know that."

"You're right. Queen Revari takes all the heads and no prisoners."

She took his hand and led him to sit down. "Who is he?"

He sighed and rubbed his eyes. "It's King Jonah."

"Oh! King Jonah! He's a wonderful MaleForm."

He stared at her. "Oh? And what makes him so wonderful?"

"He has a reputation for being veracious and a strong sense of imperturbability. I've seen a lot of meretricious MaleForms, but I'd be surprised if he were one of them."

King Justin frowned. He knew Fawn had a gift for being perspicacious. While he fully trusted her judgment, he wasn't ready to accept King Jonah as his mother's new love interest.

"I know, but...this is my mother. And after what Beeman did, I have a hard time trusting anyone."

She patted his hand. "Why?"

"Beeman or King Belial tricked me into thinking he was a good Being. He pretended to be my friend. Playing on my kindness and using it against me isn't something I can forget. When I think of all the times I ignored my gut, it pisses me off!"

At her dumbfounded expression, he said, "Sorry. I meant it makes me angry. Beeman played me from the very beginning and I never saw it coming."

"Yes, he fooled all of us, but what does that have to do with King Jonah and Queen Revari?"

"What if he's looking to take advantage of her? You may not know this, but my mother drugged General Kron on his craft. Then she programmed it to go into the sun. Somehow, he escaped and ended up in the Averlands where King Anemi murdered him."

"Wow," said Fawn. "I didn't know. General Kron went missing when I was very young. I remember watching the media reports on the TranScreen. Everyone knew of him."

Nothing his mother did surprised her. Instead of condoning Queen Revari's actions, she applauded them. While she had no issue with the late general, her father was another story. Some males deserved to die.

"If it weren't for her, maybe that wouldn't have happened. Now his brother is making a play for her? I don't buy it, Fawn. I think he's up to something. If he were my brother, I wouldn't want to date the one who placed him on a path to destruction."

"I see what you mean and I think you have every right to be concerned about Queen Revari. But from what I saw of King Jonah, he seems honorable. Now, none of us really know what a Being is thinking or feeling. Sometimes you just have to give them a chance."

She laid her hand on his shoulder. "I know what Beeman did was wrong, but King Jonah isn't him. Do you think it's fair to hold what he did to you against him?"

He didn't want to admit she had a point.

"She's been invited to his surprise LifeCelebration," he said quietly. He looked at her out of the corner of his eye. "Do you have any gowns?"

"Me? I live at the institute. I don't have time to go to royal social gatherings, Your Highness."

He slammed his fist into his palm. "We're going to fix that. Starting now." He got up from the chair. "I'll call Marcia Blight and have her send something over. We're going to Maieman!"

"At this short notice? I don't think she'll have anything in stock! And were you invited?"

"If he invited my mom and not me, then I'll know something is off."

A knock at the door interrupted her. Two WomenForms dressed in red stood outside.

"Yes," she said. "May I help you?"

"Dr. Fawn Azini? Queen Revari sent us here to get you ready for King Jonah's LifeCelebration. I have your gown and Gia will do your hair and makeup." She looked up at the king. "Oh, hello, Your Highness. The queen sent your suit too. One of your soldiers took it into your bed chamber."

He preened at Fawn. "I guess that settles it! Call me when they're finished."

"But—"

"No buts," he said, pointing at her. "We have a party to go to!"

General Legend whistled at Queen Revari's reflection in the mirror. The queen turned from left to right, noting the tight bodice of the topaz gown accentuated her trim waist and ample bust.

"King Jonah's eyes will pop out of their sockets!"

She groaned and rolled her eyes. "Legend, please don't start that again. I've already told you there's no sparks between he and I!"

"So you say, but when he sees you in that, something will definitely be on and poppin!"

She dabbed a bit of perfume on her wrists. "On and poppin? Really? You? Sounding like a Human ChildForm? It's too much!"

General Legend laughed. "Well, if you don't want him, you can always let General Lyric have him. She's single now."

She whirled around. "General Lyric? She's interested in Jonah?"

The general shrugged. "I don't know, but she might be if you don't want him."

"Since when do you look after her interests, sister?"

She winked at her. "Since never. I just wanted to see that little spark you think you're hiding!"

She waved a hand at her. "Oh, you! I'm not jealous of who he decides to date!"

"Who?" asked Gallium. "Who are we speaking of, My Queen?"

"No one," she said.

"King Jonah!" said General Legend.

"King Jonah?" echoed Gallium. "General Kron's little brother? You're with him, Your Highness?"

"I'm not *with* anyone. Legend is just being her silly self!"

She eyed Gallium speculatively. "Do you hate him as you did General Kron?"

"No. It's odd, but I don't know anything about him. I don't think anyone does. He went missing some years ago, then he appeared out of nowhere and returned to Maieman. King Micah and Queen Marietta kept the news of his return a secret. She almost ended King Dubian."

"When?"

"The first time was right before she took you to Maieman to live with her. And the second was when you were locked up." he said. "She had her soldiers hoist him over a balcony."

"What? Why would she do that?"

He leaned against a wall. "She strong-armed him into releasing you, but you know how he is. After she left, he started another bogus war with Kikhani and shipped General Kron off to fight."

"Why would she do that for me?"

"I used to see her visit Queen Dellah a lot when we lived on Coldarius. They were extremely good friends." He looked from her to his wife. "What's with the fancy dresses? I rarely see you in any, My Queen."

"We are going to King Jonah's surprise LifeCelebration," said General Legend.

Her teasing smile made him frown. "What do you mean, *we*?"

"You're going too," said General Legend.

"No, I'm not," he countered.

"Yes, you are," said Queen Revari, spraying a mist of perfume on her thighs. "Justin and Fawn are going too. He'll need security."

General Legend cackled. "Why are you spraying it down there?"

Gallium groaned. "Oh please. Can you not discuss that right now? My Queen, I don't have a suit."

Queen Revari looked at General Legend and smiled. "He doesn't have a suit!" they said in unison and laughed.

Astonished, he looked at his sneaky wife. "You ordered one for me?"

She raised both hands in the air. "Yes!"

He hung his head in defeat.

"You should get dressed, General Barrios," said Queen Revari. "Time's a ticking!"

He saluted her and shook his head when the sisters erupted in laughter again.

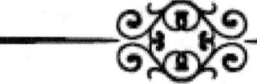

King Asa's eyes drank in Queen Vivant's beauty. "I'll be the most hated king there," he declared.

An amused smile lit up her face. "Why?"

He moved a lock of her hair off her cheek. "You'll be on my arm. There's not a king there who won't wish he could sample those juicy lips."

Blushing, she touched her lips with the tip of her finger. "Not Jonah. He doesn't have those kind of feelings for me."

"I thank The One," he muttered.

His look of uneasiness made her wary.

"Did something happen between you two?"

"No, Jonah and I are good. I think his mind will be on someone else tonight."

"My sister. I knew it! Teenah will be so happy once she finds out!"

He laughed. "Are they ready?"

On cue, the princesses came running down the stairs.

"Triplets! Slow down! I don't want you to fall in those heels!"

"No worries, Mother. Aunt Reve taught us how to run in them," said Princess Tarah.

She quirked an eyebrow. She didn't doubt it. Although the heels on her daughter's shoes were much shorter, her sister could beat half the galaxy's WomenForms in a race in nine-inch heels without breaking a sweat.

King Asa bowed to them. "You look lovely, triplets. I'm honored to escort you to Maieman."

The sisters looked at each other and blushed, even Princess Tarah.

He clapped his hands together. "Are we ready?"

The happy WomenForms all nodded.

"Then let us go!"

Queen Marietta stood in the center of the ballroom, giving orders to the dining and decorating staff. It was her son's thirtieth summer—the end of his twenties. She wanted everything to be perfect.

"Mary, I'd like the lobster tails to sit next to the crab legs, and, Fauna, please place the crab deviled eggs on the table with the cold salads. Thank you."

Mary Foxwaith smiled at her. "My Queen, we've been preparing LifeCelebration meals for generations. You've always trusted us before. Is there something we can do to ease your fears?"

The queen waved her hand a bit. "No, Mary. It's just... I've been worried about Jonah. When he was young he started getting these dreadful headaches. They started getting worse after Micah passed. He says he's fine, but I know in my heart something is going on. A MotherForm always knows when something is wrong with her ChildForm."

Mary took her arm and guided her over to a high-backed, plush chair. "My Queen, we're going to show up and show out for our king. I was there when he was born. As the head of your dining chamber, you know I'd never let him come to shame."

Queen Marietta gently patted her arm. "Yes, I know, Mary, and I thank you. He's been so lost without Lucian and his father. I just want him to be happy again. Even if it means..."

Mary pursed her lips. She knew who the queen was referring to, yet kept silent.

"I remember how it was back then, Your Highness. I think no matter how much turmoil we experience in our lifespans, we can always heal from it. That's what I was taught when I was young. Love isn't supposed to hurt."

Queen Marietta looked up at her. "It's not supposed to, but I don't think my friend, Queen Dellah, would've agreed with you. I remember attending her wedding. She was so optimistic about the future. Who would've guessed so many tragedies would happen?"

"Yes, Your Majesty, we've had some very sad times. But I'm confident things will change for the better. King Jonah is such a kind soul. He deserves all the joy and peace his heart can hold."

"Yes, he does. All right, I'll sit here and won't say a word unless I need to!"

Mary returned her. "Nonsense. Lead the way, Your Highness."

Queen Marietta monitored the decoration staff rolling out fancy topaz tablecloths she'd stitched on the highly polished marble tables. Before she knew it, the ballroom was decorated so beautifully, it made her eyes glisten with tears.

The dining staff set out a vast selection of wine, juice, and freshly brewed, sparkling blue ginger ale—Maieman's signature drink.

The tables were overloaded with appetizers of crawfish beignets, creamy crab dip, crab salad, various egg dishes, parsnip latkes accompanied by a smoky Romesco sauce, salmon croquettes, shrimp and sun-dried tomato skewers, and grilled coconut shrimp with shishito peppers.

The wide buffet style set up offered scallops seared in browned butter and lemon sauce, sole meunière, lamb haleem, braised blood orange duck legs, miso-butter roast chicken with acorn squash panzanella, filet of beef bourguignon, lamb tangine, chicken and potato gratin in brown butter cream, and roast leg of lamb with mint sauce.

A colorful array of dishes included thyme risotto, broccolini sauteed in butter, eggplants stuffed with ricotta and porcini mushrooms, portobello parmesan tagliolini, creamy polenta with black tomato and red wine ragout, leeks and shallots braised in white wine, fluffy Chantilly potatoes, green beans sauteed in olive oil and garlic, and mascarpone mashed potatoes.

The dessert tables shone with mont blanc chocolate pavlova and brown sugar pavlovas with caramelized peaches, mini chocolate-covered strawberry cheese pies, chocolate trifle with orange curd pudding, grilled pound cake with flambéed cherries and pineapples and topped with sugared almonds, blueberry lavender cheese pie, and dark chocolate tarts with braised apricots.

The grandest star of the show was King Jonah's ten-layer lemon cake frosted in glistening Italian meringue buttercream. The chrome and blue chairs were the perfect complement next to the chic elegance of the tablecloths. Short and tall glassware were lined up next to fine, sparkling china dishes and platinum cutlery wrapped in silky robin's egg blue linen napkins.

When they were finished, all of the staff lined up to bow to their queen, who stood and gave them a round of applause.

"Well done!" she said. "This will make my son so happy! I thank you all for your outstanding work."

The first guests to arrive were King Levi and his snooty wife, Apponia. Queen Marietta wrinkled her nose before letting her expression dissolve into one of a gracious hostess. She hadn't wanted to invite them, but since he had a high position, it would've been poor etiquette not to. Not to mention they would've whined about it to anyone who would've listened.

"King Levi, Queen Apponia, welcome to my home. Please help yourself to the refreshments."

A dining staff served a round of ChayBray wine for the guests to consume.

"I've been wanting to visit Maieman again since King Micah died," said Queen Apponia. "It's nice to see you're still holding up. I would've expected you not to be able to leave your bed chamber from grief. But you spent so many years together. It was time for one of you to go, right?"

King Levi sputtered and choked on his drink before casting a startled glance at his wife. Queen Marietta's cool gaze cut her up so evenly, the silly WomanForm didn't realize what she'd said was inappropriate until it was too late.

"Oh." Her nervous little laugh sounded practiced. "That sounded so mean! I'm so sorry! What I meant to say was—"

Queen Marietta's sweet tone belied the fire blazing in her eyes. "I can only guess what you meant to say, Apponia. Please refrain from touching the cake until my son slices it. I remember hearing you hid under a cake table from King Levi's first wife. She tried to gut you like a pig after finding you in her bed. I wouldn't want you to have a flashback."

The queen shook her head in admiration. "She was a real one." Savoring Queen Apponia's outraged expression, she added, "I guess waiting for Beings to die is something you've honed down to a science."

She left her guests standing red-faced and furious. The next to arrive were Queen Vivant and her ensemble. Sergeant Domi trailed behind with a half-dozen of King Asa's soldiers. King Justin and his soldiers were the last to enter.

"I don't see my mother," said King Justin.

"Oh, she'll be here with my wife and some of the Revaltians. She specializes in making grand entrances at the last minute. Let's get some champagne. If I have to be at a stuffy celebration, I might as well enjoy the spirits."

"We don't drink," said King Justin. "Fawn, would you like something that doesn't have alcohol?"

"I'd love some virgin ChayBray wine if they have it," she said.

"I think they do." He looked down at her. "You're not on call tonight, Colonel. Let Dr. Chirp and Dr. Clint take care of things. You know they're good at what they do."

"Everything looks so beautiful, I wouldn't dream of leaving early. Being invited to a royal celebration is a treat!"

He tucked a lock of her hair back in place. "You should get used to it. Pretty soon, you'll be my queen."

Thinking of their wedding made her smile. "Have you seen Queen Vivant? I don't think I could ever look so stunning!"

A hush fell over the ballroom. Everyone turned to see who had entered. They weren't disappointed by the stunning picture she made. She surveyed most of the guests with disdain, yet tossed smiles to Queen Vivant and the princesses.

King Asa earned a scowl before she rolled her eyes so hard, he hoped they rolled right out of her head. Unconsciously, Queen Apponia took a step back when her gaze zeroed in on her.

You silly adulterous whore, thought Queen Revari.

"Nonsense," she said confidently. "I don't want to hear you down yourself again, Colonel Azini. I'm sure Justin doesn't want to hear it either. Pretty soon, you'll be a part of my family. None of us are ugly ducklings."

"Yes, Your Highness," said Fawn. "You look amazing!"

"Thank you, but By The One, I can't wait until you start calling me Mother."

General Legend smiled at her. "We'll have to build your confidence, Fawn."

"Thank you, General. You look amazing too! I could use all the help I can get."

"Hello, Mother. Wow. You came dressed to kill, huh?"

Her curled. "In a manner of speaking."

When Colonels Sheila and Angela entered, King Justin did a double-take when he saw Colonel Angela's gown. He wouldn't have taken the iron-tough soldier to wear anything except a military uniform.

Reading his expression, she said, "I clean up pretty well when I want to, Your Highness."

"I agree, Colonel! I have a hunch this is going to be an evening filled with surprises!"

"Oh yes," said Queen Revari, catching General Lyric's gaze. "This will be a night none of us will ever forget!"

Chapter 6

T he musicians played softly as more guests spilled into the palace over the course of an hour. Queen Marietta didn't want to seem nervous, but she expected King Jonah a half-hour earlier. She discreetly made her way to King Asa.

"King Jonah isn't here yet. He said he was going to escort the last ChildForm we had at Bêl to their new home and would return. Has he contacted you?"

"No, Your Highness. But don't worry, I told him we were having guests at my home. He took the suit you ordered for him with him, so I'm sure he'll shower and change on the—"

Sgt. Lynn approached them. "My Queen," she said. "General Raymond has notified me the king's craft has landed! He's here!"

She clapped her hands together. "Thank you, Sgt. Lynn. Everyone! May I have your attention please? My son is headed this way with General Beaufleur! Please don't make a sound until he comes through the main entrance. Mary, would you turn out the lights, please?"

"Yes, My Queen!"

"It's so quiet, General Raymond. It hasn't been this way since my father passed."

"Sometimes we have to be grateful for the smallest of blessings, My King. If it's quiet, that means there's no emergency to attend to."

"Unless...something has happened to Mother."

"Whoa. Why would you think that, My King? If something happened to the queen, we would've been notified by now."

"I don't know. It's just... Ever since I lost Father, I panic whenever I have to leave her alone."

When they reached the entrance, General Raymond said, "I wouldn't worry. I think your evening is about to get better."

He stepped back as the king scanned his hand across the TeleShield.

"Hey, where are you going?"

The general smiled. "We're on heavy security detail. But if you need me to go inside with you, I can."

Confusion marred King Jonah's face. That only made his number one soldier smile harder. He nodded his head toward the door.

"Let us go, Your Highness."

King Jonah shook his head and went inside.

"HAPPY THIRTIETH SUMMER, KING JONAH!" the crowd shouted. "A LONG LIFE TO THE KING!"

He stood stock still, staring at over five hundred guests in attendance. Queen Marietta stood at the top of the elaborate spiral staircase, smiling down at him.

"Welcome to a celebration of your life, my dear son!"

He held back tears when his mother and their guests began singing to him. Since he'd been a sickly ChildForm, his LifeCelebrations were small, intimate moments celebrated with his parents and brother.

Later, Princess Revari had joined them. On the day of his sixteenth summer, he woke up to find her gone. Her absence had left him so deeply traumatized, he'd refused to have future LifeCelebrations.

"I—uh—" His voice faltered, then faded. "I don't know what to say! Mother, when did you do all of this for me?"

Queen Marietta descended the stairs toward him. She grabbed one of his hands and faced the crowd. "Oh, I had plenty of time while you were away. I was honored to do it. Look, King Jonah, a bounty of family, friends, and your colleagues have gathered to celebrate your thirtieth summer! I'm so thankful to The One for blessing you with another year of life!"

"Hear, hear!" said Sgt. Lynn, raising her glass.

King Jonah turned and looked at a grinning General Raymond. "So you were in on it, huh? Since when do we keep secrets from each other?"

General Raymond nodded toward Queen Marietta. "I've been taking orders from her since before you were born, My

King. Only a fool would make her angry, but we won't get into that now."

"Heavens, no!" said Queen Marietta. "Let's let the dead stay buried and forgotten!"

King Levi was as messy and miserable as they came. He was one of the few who remembered when the queen had tried to end King Dubian's life. Smirking, he shot a quick glance at Queen Vivant and Queen Revari, but quickly shifted his gaze when a hint of red glow entered the younger queen's eyes.

"She's so violent," whispered Queen Apponia.

"Shh!" he admonished her. "Do you want her to hear you? She'll take your head as sure as I'm standing here."

She shot him a dark look. "And of course you wouldn't challenge her if she did, would you, my brave husband?" she asked dryly.

"Settle down, dear. Let's just enjoy the show. With all of these overinflated egos in one chamber, there's bound to be drama tonight. I intend to enjoy every moment of it!"

The insufferable pair, joined together in unholy misery, smiled evilly at each other.

"Don't let it bother you, Revari," said Queen Vivant. "We'll be paying for Father's mistakes long after our great-grandchildren become AdultForms."

King Asa gently squeezed her hand. "Not if I have anything to say about it," he whispered in her ear.

She returned the squeeze.

"I don't care about Father's tainted legacy," said Queen Revari. "I just don't like being sneered at by King Levi and his whore. The gall of her."

Queen Vivant smiled sweetly. "Don't worry. We'll get her back."

When she nodded toward a display of amphibians in the corner, Queen Revari's radiant smile matched her sister's.

"I want everyone to eat well and enjoy themselves. We'll have supper before sampling sweet delicacies and the fabulous cake our staff made for King Jonah! Be prepared to show off your best dance moves. The music is lively tonight! Welcome everyone!"

Everyone cheered while King Jonah escorted his mother to the head table and pulled out her chair before taking a seat next to her. The servers, decked out in fancy royal blue and topaz uniforms, began escorting the guests to their assigned tables. Queen Vivant, Queen Revari, and their entourages were seated at the king's table.

Queen Revari started to sit next to Queen Vivant when a dining staff approached her and bowed. "Your Highness, the king has requested that you sit at his right side."

Her eyebrow shot up at the same time as her hand discreetly went behind General Legend's arm. The general's cheeks puffed up after feeling a soft pinch. When King Jonah stood and reached for her, the chamber became so silent, you could hear a pin drop. Taking a shaky breath, she noted Queen Vivant's hopeful expression and took his hand, allowing him to seat her at his side.

Queen Marietta inclined her head. "Queen Revari, you look ravishing tonight."

"Thank you, Queen Marietta," said Queen Revari, a bit embarrassed by the attention.

"There was a time when you called me Mother."

If Queen Revari was surprised, she didn't show it.

"Perhaps we'll get back to that in time," said Queen Marietta.

Queen Revari looked from her to King Jonah's happy, handsome face and concentrated on the food being served. She saw King Justin, Gallium, and the JanIans sitting at a table in a far corner of the room and frowned.

"King Jonah," she whispered. "Why is King Justin sitting so far from everyone?"

"I don't know. I didn't know Mother was throwing a gathering for me. Mother, do you know?"

Queen Marietta passed a platter of duck to King Jonah. "It's the only table we could sit facing the entrance of the chamber. I thought he would appreciate not having someone sitting behind him."

"You think someone would ambush him here, with me and Legend and Gallium sitting here?"

"I do," said Queen Marietta. "Not everyone is honorable, Queen Revari. As the daughter of a ruthless tyrant, no one knows that better than you. I have my son, so I'm well aware of how fiercely a mother loves her ChildForm. But no one outside of your family will ever accept King Justin for what he is."

Queen Revari fought to keep her voice low and steady. "What he is, Queen Marietta, is my son."

The older queen's tone matched hers. "A half-Human one. He'll never be allowed to forget it nor will he be forgiven for it. You were too young to understand the ramifications of your actions. King Jonah and I are prepared to protect you with our last breath. I only hope you'll understand how relentless his enemies will be."

"Of course I do, and thank you, but I don't need protection. I'm not a young, helpless female anymore. I can handle whoever comes for me. And my son."

"We're aware of that but we'll still be there if the time comes," said King Jonah. "You say you don't need me, and that's fine, but it won't stop me from trying to protect you."

He glanced at King Justin whispering in Fawn's ear. "I think it was a smart idea to seat him with his back toward the wall. With Gallium at his side, I don't think anyone would try anything, but it's better to be safe than sorry. Now, since you're fond of lamb and potatoes, would you like to share a plate with me?"

When she smiled at him, he felt as if someone had clobbered him over the head with a brick.

"I think we're being served enough to have separate plates. Thank you."

She'd die before she'd admit how intoxicating his smile was.

"Now I know what to wish for when I blow out my candles."

"Wish for good health and a long and happy life," she told him.

"Is that what you'd wish for?"

She focused on adding bright, leafy greens next to the lamb on her plate. "I haven't had a LifeCelebration since I was fifteen."

He nodded. "I remember. It was the last one you celebrated here with us. Your LifeDay is next month. Perhaps we should continue with bringing back traditions."

The Chantilly potatoes felt like decadent clouds in her mouth. "My army is too busy for unimportant things."

"Nothing about you is insignificant to me, Queen Revari. If you give me a chance, I'll spend the rest of my life proving it to you."

The low timbre of his voice tied her stomach in knots.

"The creamed broccolini is particularly good," she said. "The staff sauteed it in brown butter. I think it added more depth of flavor."

He sampled the dish, nodding his head in agreement. He knew her almost better than she knew herself. Respectfully taking her signal that she didn't want to talk about her upcoming LifeDay didn't discourage the excitement coursing through him.

However, if she thought he would abandon his plans to spoil her, she was mistaken. He intended to give her everything she would've received had she married him instead of a Human. Princess Teenah and Queen Vivant's heads were tilted toward them, trying to catch every word.

Amused by their nosiness, King Asa took a sip of sweet PotterBerry wine and shook his head. "You two are hilarious!"

"What?" asked Queen Vivant. He laughed when she winked at him.

The celebratory feast went into its second hour before Queen Marietta tapped a shiny fork against a glass.

"Now that I have your attention, it's time for dessert! Mary, we'll see the cake now, please."

Everyone oohed and ahhed when King Jonah's cake appeared. It rolled on a sophisticated robotic cart and stopped in front of him. He rose and stepped around the long table to see it more clearly.

"Is it lemon?"

"Of course," said Queen Marietta.

King Jonah smiled and winked at her. "Thank you, Mother."

"It was my pleasure."

When thirty candles were lit, he closed his eyes and said a prayer before blowing them out.

"I want to thank you all for coming to share my thirtieth LifeDay with me. It's not something I expected, and I haven't always had many close friends. But looking at all of you tonight, I can say I'm finally content with where my life is going. Not only am I hoping for my dreams to come true, but all of yours as well. Thank you."

The crowd clapped as he took his seat. The dining staff cut the cake and handed the king the first slice. Queen Marietta was served next, then Queen Revari until everyone seated at his table was served.

Queen Revari noted King Justin's table would be served last and fought to hide her dismay. Fully aware her enemies were watching her every move, she refused to give them a show.

Her son soundlessly caught her attention and smiled. He felt her discomfort and wanted to reassure her he wasn't bothered by the snub. She smiled back, almost apologetically.

She had wanted him in the universe with her so badly, she hadn't realized it may have been difficult for him to bear the brunt of the stigma Galactic Beings had against Humans. It pleased her he could handle anything they threw at him. She couldn't have been prouder.

"How's the cake, Queen Revari?" asked King Jonah.

"It's delicious. I can't remember when I've had cake this good. Oh wait. It was right after King Dubian died. We had cake then too."

He laughed.

Taking another bite of cake, she said, "What?"

"I don't think there's anyone like you in the whole galaxy. I can't tell you how refreshing it is."

"I'm glad someone thinks that."

"Me too," he said, setting his fork aside as music filled the air. "Shall we dance?"

"Dance? I don't know how to dance!"

"Sure you do! You once danced on my father's feet all the time. He and Mother taught you." He took her hand into his. "Sometimes memories return when we least expect them. Upsy-daisy!"

Before she knew it, he was leading her out on the enormous dance floor for all to see. Astonishment flooded her face when she realized she could keep up with his expert moves. Lost in their own world, neither saw the knowing looks or heard the soft whispers while they danced below the stars.

"You have to admit," said Princess Tyre, "they look pretty good together."

"Yes, they do," said Princess Tarah. "Aunt Reve looks so beautiful when she's not cutting Beings into pieces."

King Asa took Queen Vivant's hand, followed by King Justin and Fawn, with Gallium and General Legend in tow. In no time, dozens of couples had joined King Jonah and Queen Revari on the dance floor.

When the music picked up a beat, Princess Teenah and the younger Beings headed toward the sound, swaying their hips and popping their fingers. The older AdultForms stepped back when they tried to take over the floor.

Not to be denied, King Jonah challenged her by keeping up with the moves. Loud chants for the king and princess on both sides sounded throughout the chamber. Clapping their hands, everyone joined in, dancing together, keeping in rhythm with the music.

Queen Marietta surveyed the festivities from the sidelines, thoroughly enjoying herself. When they grew tired of dancing, she directed everyone's attention to an enormous display table loaded with gifts. King Jonah began opening them like a ChildForm on JehovRi.

He received golf clubs, riding gear, expensive hand-carved razors, and dozens of various items: clothing, shoes, and jewelry. One gift made him catch his breath. He looked up at Queen Marietta.

"This is Father's BrainStaff! But this was supposed to go to—"

"Yes, and now it's yours. You earned one by default, but I think it's well past time it was passed on to you. I know you'll take good care of it."

He held the chrome and topaz symbol of power in the air for all to see. The next gift was an exquisite watch and an extravagant signet ring. Made of platinum and white gold, they sparkled under the low lights of the chamber. The ring was engraved with an elaborate topaz J in the center.

King Jonah whistled. "Wow! Who spent this amount of funds on poor little old me?" He read the inscription and smiled before winking at Queen Revari. "Ah. Well... Thank you very much. I'll cherish these until all of this," he raked his hand through his thick black hair, "is gray!"

King Justin saw the happiness in his mother's eyes and frowned. At the same time, King Jonah's eyes found his. Before he could react, King Justin saw his eyes turn as black as a raven. A sharp pain coursed through his skull, and then—nothing! A few moments passed before he could focus again. Someone was calling him.

"King Jonah? King Jonah?"

When he glanced at King Justin again, he was looking at him suspiciously.

King Asa cleared his throat, bringing King Jonah out of his reverie. He shook his head a bit before flashing a smile. "Yes, Mother? I'm sorry, I'm just so thunderstruck by these gifts, I lost myself for a moment."

Just then, the clock struck three a.m. and the guests began to rise and say their goodbyes. He sighed with relief when he saw them streaming out of the palace.

"Oh, King Jonah, tonight was grand!" exclaimed Queen Vivant. "I don't remember when I've had so much fun!"

"I'm glad you came, sister. Teenah is quite the little performer, isn't she?"

She laughed. "That she is! Honestly, I don't know where she gets it from. Lucian and I made a solemn couple. I never saw him dance."

His eyes shone. "Oh, he was quite a dancer! He had no time for it after he came to Platirius. There wasn't much to be joyful about, you know."

Her smile slightly faltered. "I wish things could've been different."

"It's all right, Vivant. We're still alive and we're all together. I'd like to think he and Father are smiling down on us. They might've even danced with us tonight!"

She gave him a hug. "I thank Mother for letting us share your LifeCelebration with you and I'm proud of you for appreciating it."

"I didn't have a choice, remember? It was quite a surprise."

King Asa approached with her coat and helped her put it on. "We'll have to do this again sometime. We work hard to protect our realms. We might as well play hard too."

"I agree!" said King Jonah.

Queen Revari and General Legend were the next to appear. "King Jonah, we had a good time. Thank you for inviting us."

"I appreciate that, but thank Queen Marietta. I was a guest too, you know."

They all laughed.

His eyes ravished her. "Are you staying for tea? Mother had the dining staff create a special blend just for you."

"No, she isn't," said King Justin, approaching with his party. He turned to Queen Revari. "Mom, we're re-decorating some chambers in the west wing of the palace. I'd like your expertise on a color palette, if you wouldn't mind spending the week's end with Fawn and I? Aunt Legend, you're welcome to come too."

"I'd love to," said Queen Revari. "Good night, King Jonah. A long and happy life to you."

She left with General Legend and the Revaltians marching in front of and behind her.

King Justin's mocking gaze swept over his face.

"I'll be right out, Gallium and Colonel Lionus."

"Yes, My King," said Gallium.

He resisted the urge to knock the sneer off King Justin's face. "What's the matter, King Jonah? You look disappointed. I guess you won't be putting your lips on my mother's behind tonight, eh?"

"Where I put my mouth is none of your business."

King Justin took a step toward him. "When my mother is involved, it's my business 24/7. Now, I appreciate you helping General Lyric and assisting us with King Anemi. But my mother is off limits to you."

He laughed. "Who are you to tell me what's off limits to me, Human? You act as if you belong here, but you don't have any friends outside JanIus. Queen Vivant has to tolerate you because she loves Revari, and Princess Tarah tolerates you out of dutiful love for her mother. But don't think I can't turn her or her sisters against you. I'm their uncle. And you? You're worth less than the shit we flush."

"Ahhh, now we see the real King Jonah, yeah? How about I tell my mother what you just said. How long do you think you'll be in her good graces?"

"About as long as it would take for King Asa to take your head after I tell him what you did to Queen Vivant. He hates you. We all hate you. You may be the great-grandson of King Carlomon, but you're also linked with King Dubian, whom everyone despised. If I unleash Asa on you, he won't hesitate to cut you down and take JanIus. Then where would your little doctor be?"

Checking his surroundings, King Justin forced himself to remain calm.

"If I were you, I'd think of her and all the poor souls on JanIus who have no choice but to depend on a nasty little half-Human for their survival. I don't think you have any room to threaten me, and this had better be the last time you do."

General Raymond stepped forward when he spit on the ground. "Get your ass out of my palace."

A furious King Justin stepped around them to leave.

"And fix your face. If Revari finds out about this little conversation, JanIus will be conquered and Dr. Azini will be sold to the most misogynistic king I can find."

King Justin turned to him. "Don't ever threaten her again!"

"I just did, Human. You're a king in name only. An unwanted perversion among our realms. You'll never have the same level of respect as the rest of us."

His steps toward the outraged king were slow and deliberate. "You'd better learn your place. If not"—he gestured toward General Raymond—"we don't mind teaching you. Get in my way to Revari again, I'll take your head myself."

"I have a big head, Your Highness. Make sure your swords are sharper than your threats."

General Raymond's jaw clenched. "If he wants trouble, we'll give him all he can stand, Your Highness."

He stared at King Justin until he disappeared in the darkness. "Trouble. That's the magic word, General."

Queen Apponia giggled. "Did you see the way King Jonah and that Human looked at each other? The hate nearly radiated off them!"

"Yes, I think the Human definitely sent a challenge to King Jonah. One that he's going to lose!"

"It was clever of Queen Marietta to seat him the way she did. She knew none of us wanted to be close enough to smell him!"

King Levi undid a couple of buttons on his shirt. "Queen Marietta has always stood on propriety. No one could accuse her of ignoring proper etiquette. I'm surprised she invited him."

"Then she would've had to deal with Queen Revari's antics. She's been childish for as long as I've known her. I think Queen Marietta did it to save face. After all, she loves Queen Vivant much more than she could ever love her!"

He turned down the comforter on the bed. "Hm. Yes, that's true. She can't contend with one without the other clinging to her heel. If King Micah and General Kron were alive, things would be different.

He exiled Revari from social circles. King Jonah wants to get inside her panties—nothing more. Once he's finished with her, he'll toss her like a frog that climbed out of the swamp."

Queen Apponia fluffed her pillows. "I can't imagine being desperate enough to allow a filthy Human to place his hands all over me. She should've swept the babe away before she returned to Platirius." She turned to him. "You know, I'll never understand how he escaped King Dubian. I grew up believing he'd sent him into the sun."

"It sounds as if treachery was at play," said King Levi. "I've always suspected Queen Revari orchestrated his escape and deceived her father. He should've ended her the minute she was dragged back to Platirius." He pulled the covers up to his chin. "I doubt we'll ever know the real story. That family thrives on secrets."

She added a few drops of lavender essential oil to the sheets. "Hm. My money is on King Jonah. He may be less ruthless than General Kron, but I've always said it's the quiet ones you have to watch! That Human had better watch his back or his head will be severed and JanIus will be in the hands of a real king!"

King Levi looked at her. "And what makes you think that honor doesn't belong to me?"

She waved a hand at him. "Please, Levi. We both know you let your soldiers fight for you. You would have to be close enough to him to take his head." She patted his knee. "You're much too cowardly for that." She turned around. "Now help me get out of this gown!"

"Hurumph! Thanks for your vote of confidence!" He eyed something moving in the gown. "What's that?"

She whirled around. "What are you talking about?"

Cautiously, he rolled up a wad of heavy paper and smacked her on the back.

"Oh, for heaven's sakes, Levi—"

She screamed when a large lizard crawled out of her gown. Her screams rang out into the star-filled night while her husband roared with laughter.

"Someone put a lizard in your dress when you weren't looking!"

"Quiet, you useless disgrace!" she screamed, backing away from the bed. "Get it out of here!"

Comfortably perched on her pillow, the lizard looked at her and flicked his tongue.

Q ueen Marietta stared out at the moon for a long time. She should've been in bed an hour ago, but something kept nagging her.

Something significant happened between Jonah, Asa, and the Human tonight. But what?

For a split second, the dynamics had changed between the three, but for the life of her, she couldn't figure it out. And it worried her. Her intuition told her whatever she missed wasn't to be taken lightly. Or ignored.

H e finished the spell and lay back against the covers, sweat covering his naked body. The Human must be stopped. He was willing to do anything to make it happen. No matter who got in his way, nothing would stop his plans from coming to fruition. Especially King Justin.

They entered the palace and headed toward their bed chambers. As King Justin escorted his mother to her chamber, he kept up a cheerful façade so that she wouldn't notice how upset he was. Hell bent on keeping King Jonah away from her, his emotions were all over the place.

The psychotic bastard! He pretends to be a boy scout, but underneath, he's as crazy as a serial killer! I could kill him for threatening Fawn!

Queen Revari peered into his face. "What's bothering you?"

He knew better than to lie to her.

"I don't like the idea of you dating King Jonah. I think you can do better. Much better!"

She laughed. "We're not dating. We've known each other for my whole life. No need to worry about him."

But he did worry. More than he was willing to let her know. He planted a soft kiss on her forehead.

"Here we are. Sleep well. I've asked the dining staff to serve some of your favorites for breakfast."

"Thank you for thinking of me."

"I always will, Mama. Always."

Chapter 7

He found Queen Marietta standing in the middle of King Micah's old den. Perusing the endless rows of books on evil spells and dark magic, she sucked her teeth.

"I nearly fainted when Micah told me he'd once been a sorcerer. I suspect he'd have lived longer if he hadn't been involved in it. But it was a time before he met me, so who was I to judge?"

She turned to face him. "I understand you're an adult now and you don't need me as much anymore, but I beg you not to follow down this path. There's nothing worth shaving years off of your life and dying before your time."

He glanced at a shelf above her head and sat on the edge of the desk. "I intend to marry Revari and merge peacefully with Revani. But I also want to get rid of the Human and take JanIus. That takes an enormous amount of power. Once both realms are under my command, Maieman will be equal to Platirius."

She sat down. "I've never heard you voice such ambition before."

A flicker of something she didn't recognize appeared in his eyes.

"Sitting on the throne wasn't part of my plans, but it's done now. Had Lucian not been robbed of his destiny, he would've been Platirius's king. This family would've been the most powerful in all the realms. If my plans succeed, it'll happen despite King Anemi's actions."

Folding his arms across his chest, he said, "Don't you see? After Lucian defeated King Hitam twice, King Dubian ruled the galaxy unchecked for years. He used Maieman to stay on top. Then came his order for banishment to that dark hole, Ziltach."

He kneeled to her. "How many years did he cause you to lose with your sons? Now? I'll have his daughter, his old enemy's planet, and the descendants of the planet he destroyed. It's the perfect revenge against Platirius's old kings. If I succeed, the descendants of your descendants will have immeasurable wealth and power."

She folded her hands on her lap. "And what of Platirius?"

"What of it? I have no interest in it—that's King Asa's goal. He and Vivant can have its power and its ghosts while we'll have equal power." He looked up at a painting of King Micah. "I think he would be proud of all I've done for the family."

"He would be. And so am I. Tell me something. Are you in love with Revari?"

"Yes. For a while I'd forgotten how deep my feelings were for her, but when I'm with her, I feel normal."

She cocked her head. "What do you mean, normal?"

He swallowed. "She alleviates my anxiety. It's difficult for me to make friends. Always has been. And I'm not a confrontational

MaleForm. But when she's next to me, I'm bolder, more confident and braver. As if I can take on anyone and anything that stands in my way."

She laid a hand on his broad shoulder. "Then you have my blessing. I think you both need each other to heal and to grow. It's a chance to pick up where you left off before Revari changed her life by aligning herself with the Humans. She's still a very young WomanForm. You could have babies and raise a family. You have my full support, son. But please find another way to conquer JanIus without sorcery."

She rose from the chair. "The gains aren't worth the risk, Jonah. Micah and I reared you and Lucian to be honorable. Take it from me, a ruler sleeps better at night when his conscience is clear."

"You're a wise ruler in your own right. I'll keep that in mind."

She kissed his cheek. "I'm going to lie down for a nap. It's your turn to choose the supper menu. Please don't have my heart burning with anything too spicy!"

Spicy?

"Sleep well."

He dispatched the cleaning staff to the den.

"Remove every book about magic and take them to an incinerator to burn. Make sure you get all of them. Leave the rest."

"Yes, King Jonah."

A fully clothed General Legend laid on Queen Revari's bed. "I'm so restless. We haven't had a battle in quite a while!" She lay back on the soft covers and sighed. "I'm ready for some action!"

Queen Revari looked at her through the mirror while she pinned up her hair. "I'm ready for you to get your bouncy DingoPops off my bed!"

General Legend smiled sweetly. "Why? Is King Jonah's scent on your sheets?" She pressed her nose into a pillow. "Nope! Still smells like you—sugar cookies and vanilla beans!"

Queen Revari laughed. "You know, sometimes it's really hard to believe you're the older sister."

The general stood up and swung her hips from side to side. "And I look so GOOD too!" She looked over at the queen. "This is just my opinion, but I don't think you should lift your hair off your shoulders."

Queen Revari reached for another pin. "Why?"

"It makes you look like Queen Opal. She was the polar opposite of Queen Dellah. She never let her hair fall past her shoulders."

She laughed again. "I have her face, Legend. I don't think there's much I can do about that."

General Legend's playful mood turned solemn. "She hated me you know."

"Aunt Opal hated you? Why?"

"She wanted Gallium to be her lover."

Her hand slowly left her hair. "My Aunt Opal wanted to bed Gallium?!"

"Her and most WomenForms in the galaxy. You look shocked, sister."

"Well...I am. She was always so prim and proper. She didn't seem like the type to...you know...want to get down and dirty under Gallium." Suddenly, she turned around to face General Legend. "Was my mother in love with him too?"

"I don't think so. You must understand, My Queen, no one dared to discuss Queen Dellah. They were too afraid of setting King Dubian off and that wasn't hard to do. She and Gallium were really close friends, but for many years, she was in love with your father. I'll always be grateful to her for not choosing Gallium to be at her side. I was definitely no competition for her. No one was."

"Aunt Opal and Gallium," she murmured, shaking her head in wonderment. "I can't imagine it. I've always seen him as a father figure." She let down her long hair. "FatherForms aren't sexy."

"He is to meeeeeee," sang General Legend.

Queen Revari playfully tossed a pin at her. "I should hope so! You married him!"

"Yeah, that was a beautiful ceremony." She shot the queen a sly look. "I've been waiting for you, you know."

Queen Revari dragged a brush through her curls. "Why?"

"To see you in a long white gown carried by dozens of tiny ChildForms as you float toward a handsome, honorable king."

She put the brush down. "You'll be waiting a long time for that!"

The general fastened platinum butterfly clips in her hair. "No reason I should have to when you have one right in front of you."

The queen threw up her hands. "First Vivant, then my nieces, and now you? All of my warriors like him—even Jia melts when he passes! What is it about King Jonah that makes you all go cow-eyed over him?"

General Legend put on one of the queen's hats and danced around the bed chamber. "He's handsome and dashing!"

After finishing the dance, she held the hat away from her body as if waiting for applause. "But underneath all that, he's phlegmatic—he doesn't readily fly off the handle like someone I know."

Queen Revari rolled her eyes when she winked at her. "I never took you as the romantic type."

"Oh, I am. And he has other redeeming qualities too. He's stoic and his benignity reminds me of King Carlomon. You could scour the whole galaxy and not find a single Being with a bad word to say about King Jonah. Think of the beautiful babies you'd have!"

Queen Revari scoffed. "My womb is closed for business."

"Says who? We don't get menopausal like Human women! We can have as many babies as we want for as long as we choose."

A mischievous smile settled on the queen's lips. "You and Gallium should get to it then."

General Legend straightened a couple of pillows on the bed. "No way!"

"So it's okay for me to get pregnant, but not you?"

"I never wanted babies. There was a time when Gallium did, but I'm not sure if he does now."

"You haven't talked about it?"

A melancholy shadow crossed the general's face. "I'm just happy he forgave me for choosing my career over our relationship, and then for copulating with Simonius. I'm too afraid to mention it. That's a boat that doesn't need rocking."

"I get you. But Gallium loves you. He'd do anything for you. It's true you both are at different stages of your lives, but we barely age. Take your own advice: you can have babies at any time."

She gazed wistfully out the window. "The truth is, I'm afraid to open my heart again. I never had the opportunity to raise Justin. I didn't get to feed him or see him take his first steps. When I think of all the things I was robbed of, it breaks my heart."

General Legend moved over when she approached the bed, making room for her to sit beside her. "But Oliver was so good and sweet and decent. What if I give myself to the wrong MaleForm? What if his toxicity mixes with my bloodline and we produce another generation of madness?"

"And what if you don't, My Queen? Your mind always goes to the worst pain, the worst tragedy. What if you stepped out on faith and you got to live the happy life that was taken from you? The One restores what we lose. It's one of His promises to us. 'I will give you back what you lost to the swarming locusts, the hopping locusts, the stripping locusts, and the cutting locusts. It was I who sent this great destroying army against you.' Joel 2:25."

Queen Revari chuckled ruefully. "And what an army it was. Surviving King Dubian was the toughest challenge of my lifespan."

General Legend patted her on the shoulder. "Don't give up on love. Believe me, if there's anyone who knows about staying in prayer, it's me. I never imagined I'd see Gallium look at me the way he does, but it happened. After everything I've done, he still loves me, and so does The One. Give yourself grace, Your Highness. You deserve to be loved."

She cupped her chin in her hand. "You know you don't have to be so formal when we're alone."

General Legend laid her head on her shoulder. "It's just my way of showing you respect and how proud I am of all that you've accomplished. A queen in charge of her own planet and army. Until you dealt with King Dubian, that was unheard of. You are the first WomanForm to take control of a planet. That honor will always belong to you."

Queen Revari patted her thigh. "Thank you, Legend. I appreciate you more than you know."

The TeleShield buzzed and Sergeant Tylo entered her bed chamber.

"My Queen, King Jonah is here to see you again."

She composed herself while ignoring General Legend's gleeful smile.

"Thank you, Tylo. Tell him I'll be down in a minute."

"Go get him, My Queen!" said General Legend.

"One more word out of you and I'll ship you over to Platirius."

The general's arms froze in the air. "For what?"

"All this talk about opening myself up and love and such. Don't you think it's time you and Vivant buried the hatchet?"

"I would but I'm afraid she'd bury it in my skull. Did you see her fist go through my leg?"

She examined her thigh. "Advisor TamRi patched you up so well, one would never know it happened. She wasn't herself. Sometimes trauma can make you do things you regret."

"She didn't seem remorseful at King Jonah's LifeCelebration. She refused to look at me."

Queen Revari slid her hands down her outfit, ensuring she looked her best before she met the king.

"Vivant thinks I love everyone more than her. She's always been very insecure. But I believe some things are worth praying for. Healing our family is one of them. I'll see you later."

General Legend smiled. "Oh, wait!" After spraying two quick puffs of perfume on her neck, she stood back and said, "Now you're ready! In a while, My Queen."

Queen Revari rolled her eyes to the heavens. "In a while!"

He was waiting for her at the bottom of the staircase. She noted he was more handsome than General Kron. His gaze was so amorous, she felt as if she were floating on a cloud. But she wasn't about to let him know that.

"King Jonah? To what do I owe this visit?"

"We were interrupted the night of my LifeCelebration. I was hoping to spend more time with you. Did you enjoy your visit to JanIus?"

She led him into her library and gestured for him to sit down in one of the high-backed, expensive chairs.

"I always enjoy spending time with my son."

"And how do you get along with his friend? Dr. Azini?"

"I think she's an intelligent, competent WomanForm. She's the perfect complement to Justin."

He raised an eyebrow. "As opposed to General Lyric?"

She sucked her teeth in disgust. "I'm having a grand day. Can we please not talk about her?"

"I would've thought you two might've gotten closer after her accident."

She looked at him as if he'd just announced he'd run ten laps around her palace stark naked.

"And what made you think that?"

"Because you're responsible for getting her pushed down a cliff. Lady Alarah was working for you, was she not?"

Her eyes narrowed. "Just what are you getting at, King Jonah?"

He smiled. "Don't worry. I'll never tell King Justin. I know what that would do to your relationship."

"I don't like your tone. Are you threatening me?"

"My Queen, I'd go through Hell and back to keep you safe. I'm just making you aware I know your secret and it's safe with me."

She folded her arms across her chest. "What you *think* is my secret. I have no idea what you're talking about."

When he smiled, there was something different about the way he looked at her. As if knowing the real her excited him.

"Come join me on my boat today. We'll see the sights and I'll catch dinner. I'm dying for some crabs and sea bass."

"I don't fish, Jonah. Besides, I don't like boats. All that water with nowhere to go." She shuddered. "It's suffocating."

"I do and I'm pretty good at it. You don't have to come up on the deck with me, you could stay in the cabin. It's so beautiful, you won't realize we're over water. Come on, My Queen. Come with me."

The deep timbre of his voice made her nipples tighten. After taking a vow of celibacy, she'd decided to stave off copulation. But if the heat in his gaze kept simmering, she'd have to disappoint The One.

"How long will this little trip be?"

His smile.

"All weekend."

"King Jonah," she groaned.

"I promise I won't touch you unless you ask me to. Nor will I do anything to make you uncomfortable. I just want a bit of your time, that's all. No wars are going on. We deserve to have some fun, yes?"

She got up. "All right, I'll pack a bag."

"No need for that. I have everything you need—clothing, toiletries, your favorite snacks."

"Wow, you had it all planned out, huh? And what if I had said no?"

His teasing eyes met hers. "Then I would've waited for another time."

He lifted his impressive, athletic body out of the chair and stood towering over her. Her hands going to her curvaceous hips amused him.

He stretched out his hand and said, "Shall we go?"

"Will you need us to go with you, My Queen?"

"No, Private Jio, I'll be fine, thank you."

The private handed her BrainStaff to her.

"Thank you, I never go anywhere without this!"

King Jonah inclined his head at the private, flashing a charming smile. It worked. She floated out of the library.

Queen Revari rolled her eyes. "Is there anyone in the galaxy not overwhelmed by your charm?"

Mischief gleamed in his eyes. "Does that include you?"

She sucked her teeth. "I'd like to take a couple of my favorite books."

He nodded. "Of course. I've brought a few of my own."

"What kind?"

"Historical. I want to research how the galaxy functioned in the old times. If I'm to have a successful reign, I want to make sure I pay homage to my ancestors."

"An ambitious undertaking," she said, standing on a stool to reach for a book on a high shelf. "Oh!" she cried.

He caught her in his arms, preventing her from falling backward. Before she knew it, he was cradling her like a baby, his beautiful face masked with concern.

"Are you all right? Which one did you need? I'll get it."

"Oh, for heaven's sake, I can get my own book, Jonah! I've been a bit dizzy lately."

Instinctively, he held her closer to his chest. "Dizzy? Have you seen a doctor?"

She waved off his anxiety. "I'm fine. Don't worry."

"Which book is it?" he repeated more firmly.

He set her down gently and grabbed the ones she wanted off the shelf. Taking them from him, she placed them in an oversized bag filled with candies and small bottles of water.

"I'm ready," she announced.

General Legend stood at the door. "Are you sure you don't want any of us to accompany you? It's no problem, Your Highness."

"Thank you, but no. Hold down the fort until I return."

"Yes, My Queen."

He winked at General Legend. "Don't worry, I'll take good care of her and bring her back in one piece!"

"I'm holding you to that, Your Highness."

The queen didn't see her Revaltians and all the staff in her work chambers press their noses against the windows to see she and King Jonah enter his craft. They were happy for her.

She was finally getting the love and attention she deserved. For them, King Jonah was her savior. As for her, everything was happening so fast, she didn't have time to process it.

He'd come to see why she'd taken captive of his heart. Now that he'd found the answer, he wasn't about to let her go.

She'd done the impossible in captivating him as a moth drawn to a flame. He looked forward to turning up the heat.

Several days later

King Justin was in a foul mood. He wanted to punch someone. King Jonah was at the top of his list.

He pressed a button on his desk. "Nola, has my mother returned any of my calls?"

"No, Your Highness. When she does, I'll dispatch the transmission right away!"

Disappointed, he sat back in his chair. "Thank you, Nola."

Fawn entered with two carry-out trays. "Luncheon time!" she announced. "I bought beautiful fillets of red snapper over a bed of saffron rice, creamy cabbage, and the softest rolls to ever hit your lips!"

He glanced at her cleavage.

I doubt it.

She set the container down on the table and held another one up in front of him. "Or you can have the shrimp and jalapeno and cheese grits. Mr. Alberman said he caught the shrimp this morning!"

"I'll take the shrimp and grits, thank you."

She gave the container a little shake before handing it to him. "You're welcome! Here you go, Your Highness!"

"Fawn, you're my lady now. Please stop addressing me that way."

"I'm sorry. I've tried. I really have! It's not something I can get used to."

"Will you call me that when we're old and gray?"

"We don't age like—"

She caught herself.

He smiled for the first time since he woke up. She had that effect on him.

"Like what? Humans?"

She lowered her eyes and nodded.

He reached for her hand. "It's all right. I know you didn't mean anything by it."

"I didn't, and please forgive me." She looked up at him. "I don't know if you knew but you'll age very slowly here, if at all. Are you okay with looking young forever?"

He sighed. "I think so. I don't know anyone who looks forward to graying hair and moving slower."

"Yes, but it means something else."

He lifted the top of the carton. "And what would that be?"

"Now that you've been here for a while, returning to Earth is out of the question."

"Not that I've thought of leaving JanIus, but why?"

"Our years are accelerated in the galaxy. If you return to Earth, you may be so old that you'll...die."

His head snapped up. "What?!"

She nodded. "Going to and from Earth doesn't affect us, but you're half Human. Your DNA is suspended in time here, but once you're out of the galaxy, there's no guarantee you'll live to return again."

He reared back in the chair, shaking his head. "Wow. That's good to know. Thank you for telling me, Fawn."

"Anytime. Now what's got you in such a sour mood?"

His uproarious laugh made her smile.

"Even when I try to hide my moods from you, you always pick up on them!"

"I do. It's a consequence of being raised by a liar. You learn to read body language before you trust words."

"I'm sorry you had to go through that with your father. Please know I'd never lie to you."

She unwrapped her utensils and spread a napkin across her lap. "I do."

"How's your mother?"

"Mother is mothering. She finally agreed to talk to Dr. Barbara. She's even stopped drinking."

He took a bite of shrimp and grits. "That's wonderful!"

She bit her lip. "Yes, it is. I hope it continues."

"We'll pray it does. Now that your father is gone, maybe she'll see she can have a good life without being treated worse than a dog."

The TeleShield buzzed.

"Hello? King Justin? Your assistant said I could come in."

What the hell is he doing here?

King Justin stood up. "King Jonah? How can I help you?"

His crisp tone made Fawn sit at attention. If Maieman's ruler picked up on his hostility, he didn't let it show. Instead, he smiled at her.

"Oh, hello, Dr. Azini. It's great to see you again!"

She snuck a peek at King Justin before standing and taking his outstretched hand. "I'm well, Your Highness. How are you feeling? That was quite a LifeCelebration. I've never been to a royal one before."

When he kissed her hand, King Justin fought to keep a snarl off his lips.

"I'm glad you enjoyed it. Get used to it, there'll be many more to come! In fact, Queen Revari's Life Day is next month."

He turned to King Justin. "I was wondering if you and I could team up and give her the grandest LifeCelebration she's ever seen!"

King Justin frowned at him. "Why would I want to do that?"

King Jonah shrugged. "King Dubian wouldn't allow her to have them after her aunt died. My family celebrated them with her when she lived with us—"

"My mother lived with you?" asked King Justin in disbelief. "Why?"

"King Dubian treated her atrociously. My mother grew tired of his antics and brought her home. She lived with us for years until he stole her. Then she ran away to Earth, and the rest is a sad part of history. I intend to undo all the years of pain he caused her. I can't think of a better person to help me with that than you. She loves you more than herself, you know."

Why is he acting as if he didn't threaten me at his party?

"Colonel Azini, go and enjoy your luncheon. I'll catch up with you later."

She bowed to them. "Of course, My King."

He waited until the door was closed before turning to King Jonah. "You really are a piece of work, you know that?"

"I don't know what you mean."

"You nearly took my head off at your party—"

"Par-tee?" echoed King Jonah.

"LifeCelebration," said King Justin through clenched teeth. "You threatened Fawn—"

King Jonah held up his hand. "Whoa. I would never do something like that. Dr. Azini is a kind and beautiful WomanForm. I have nothing against her. Or you."

"Were you an actor in another life?"

King Jonah pursed his lips. "No. Why?"

"You're standing there as if—"

He signed in exasperation when the TeleShield buzzed again. "Is Nola allowing the entire galaxy in here today?"

Jia, a Revaltian sorceress, entered carrying a rose-colored box.

"Your Highness, Queen Revari asked me to deliver these to you personally. It's samples of cake for you and Dr. Azini. She wants to know your choice right away so she can tell the royal baker what to bake for your wedding."

"Jia, I haven't even proposed to Fawn yet. Even if she says yes, I think my mother is jumping the gun!"

Confused, she looked from him to King Jonah, who shrugged and shook his head.

"Jumping the what?"

"She's making wedding plans too fast," explained King Justin.

"Ah, I see." She set the box down on the table. "We both know she won't take no for an answer, King Justin. Do you think the two of you could make a decision by this evening?"

King Justin sighed in frustration. "I don't think so. Let me talk to my mother, okay."

"All right." Her face lit up at King Jonah. "Hello, Your Highness!"

"Hello, Jia! It's nice to see you again! I was just stopped by to thank King Justin for coming to my LifeCelebration. I hope he'll help me plan one for the queen."

She clapped her hands in delight. "Oh, that would be wonderful! She loves flashy events!"

King Justin crossed his eyes and turned slightly away from them.

She felt the strained tension in the air. "Oh! Am I interrupting? I'll head on out."

"No, no. You stay. I have some things to do back in my realm. King Justin, I'll call you later if that's all right? In a while!"

Jia waved cheerfully at him while King Justin looked at him as if he were trash.

"Can you believe him? The gall of him thinking I'd work with him on anything."

Jia looked up at him in confusion. "Why not? He's a good king. And he's crazy about the queen."

"I think he's crazy, period. He bit my head off when we were on Maieman."

"King Jonah? He's the nicest MaleForm in the galaxy. Maybe he was tired? It was quite an event."

"What is it about him that makes everyone fall all over him? I don't get it! I don't think he's nice at all! And he's a liar! He's not interested in me helping him plan anything for my mother!"

"I don't want to step out of my place, Your Highness, but I feel when energy shifts in souls. He wasn't lying about wanting your help. I think he's sincere."

"You didn't see him right before we left the palace, Jia. You didn't hear what he said to me."

"I see. Let's pull up the transmission," she said.

To his astonishment, she waved her hand and surveillance of him and King Jonah talking at the end of the LifeCelebration appeared. His eyes grew wider when he heard the conversation between them.

"But that's impossible! That's not what we said to each other! That was a friendly conversation!"

"Yes. One that ended with him asking you to help him plan an event for the queen and you telling him to come and see you. Which is precisely what he did."

King Justin rubbed his eyes. "I don't believe this. I don't know what's going on!"

"Is it possible you've been overworking yourself? Ruling a realm isn't easy. Especially when you have no experience with it."

He opened his mouth, but no words came out. He wouldn't know what to say if he tried.

"It may not be my place to say this, but everyone makes mistakes sometimes, even royalty. King Jonah is as nice as they come and he's head over heels for my queen. Please try and get to know him. I promise you won't regret it."

She ducked her head toward the fancy box. "Try the cake. Rosalee's cakes are guaranteed to boost your mood. In a while, Your Majesty."

He sat on the table, trying to digest what happened when he heard someone laughing. He turned and saw...

D.L. HANNAH

King Dimaro!

Chapter 8

Impossible!

"How are you alive?"

The wicked king's laughter became louder and louder until King Justin bent over, his hands clasped over his ears. Then...nothing. He was gone as fast as he came. Beads of sweat popped over his face.

What the hell is going on?! He's dead!

He ran out of the chamber and found King Jonah laughing and talking with Gallium. Jia came up behind him. As they looked on, King Jonah took Gallium's outstretched hand and shook it.

"See, Your Highness? If King Jonah was a fraud, Gallium would know. My vibe is sorcery, but Gallium is one of The One's soldiers. Even the best of charlatans can't fool both the light and the dark."

Long after King Jonah's departure, trepidation held King Justin in an unrelenting grip. He wasn't clairvoyant, yet he couldn't shake the feeling that his world would come crashing down around him. Again. And this time, there would be no one to help him.

Queen Vivant gathered a few butternut squash and bok choy and added them to a large basket with some eggplants.

"What would you do if you couldn't be out here working like a gardening staff?"

She looked over her shoulder and pushed the brim of her wide hat off her face. "Revari!" she cried excitedly. "You've come to see me!"

"Yes, sister, I'm full of surprises these days."

Queen Vivant looked over her shoulder. "You didn't bring that General Legend with you, did you?"

"Of course I did, but she's at General Lyric's cottage. You know, the two of them have become closer since Lady Alarah pushed her off that cliff." She lifted an eggplant from the basket. "It would be nice if the two of you patched things up and acted like real sisters."

The frosty gleam in Queen Vivant's eyes made her say, "Or not. I've been told I look like Mother, but I swear she must've worn that look a time or two."

"Oh, she did. Many times when she was vexed." Her eyes roamed over her younger sister. "You didn't come all this way for nothing. What's bothering you? I thought Jonah was making you happy."

"He is," Queen Revari admitted quietly. "He's handsome and cultured and charming."

Queen Vivant rose to her feet, taking the basket in one hand and her sister's hand in the other. Queen Revari followed her to a small bench and sat.

"I hear a 'but' coming." She sat down beside her. "What's the matter, Revari? Is he too tame for you? I know you like MaleForms with a bit of turmoil like King Leighton. But maybe it might be better to settle down with a decent one."

"I know you want Jonah and I to get together, but I don't think it's a good idea."

She adjusted the hat and wiped the sweat from her brow. "Why?"

Queen Revari scanned her face. "If I tell you, do you promise not to laugh at me?"

Queen Vivant righted one of the butterfly clips in her hair. "Revari, I would never laugh at you! I'm your sister!"

"I think I'm cursed."

"Cursed? Why would you say that?"

"King Belial was the worst, but he hasn't been the only insane MaleForm who wanted me. The ones who are attracted to me *are* insane, Vivant."

She wrapped her arms around herself. "It's been hard to let go of Oliver because he was so wonderful—thoughtful, gentle, and mentally sound. He was the complete opposite of our father. But after he died, I realized I attract the ones who are just like King Dubian."

She looked at Queen Vivant. "I've never been lucky in love like you. Two sane MaleForms fell in love with you. I think the reason I've held on to Oliver's memory is it's the one time in my life where I had stability with a male. I didn't have to worry about him harming me."

Queen Vivant moved her long, thick, wooly hair off her shoulder. "Do you think Jonah will hurt you?"

Queen Revari sighed. "I don't think he will. My heart doesn't tell me he will, but what if he does? I don't want to give my love to someone who won't appreciate it. And there's more. There are things I can't remember. When Mother and Grandfather Carlomon restored the ones I'd lost, my memory should've been whole, but it isn't. I don't remember living on Maieman. When I try to recall what life was like there, I can't."

Queen Vivant set the basket of vegetables on the ground. "Maybe your mind is protecting you by blocking your memories."

"Yes, but from what? If living with the Krons was good for me, what happened that I don't want to remember? What happened before King Dubian stole me from them?"

Queen Vivant frowned. "I don't know but Father didn't steal you from Maieman. You returned to Platirius on your own."

"What? Why would I do that?"

"I don't know. When I woke up, you were lying next to me. You told me you didn't want to talk about Maieman and you weren't going back. You never mentioned the Krons again."

Queen Revari shook her head slowly. "That's odd."

"I agree. It is. They spoke so fondly of you, I didn't want to pry. Queen Marietta believed Father had you kidnapped. I didn't have the heart to tell her the truth."

"But what is the truth?"

Queen Vivant flicked her finger against one of the squashes. "Only you know that, Revari. Maybe Dr. Barbara can help you regain your memories. Oh, don't look at me that way! Mental wellness has changed since you were locked away. If the lapses in your memory are really bothering you, I think you should give therapy a chance. Then your memories of Maieman may return."

She squeezed Queen Revari's hand. "For better or worse, it will guide you to either move forward with Jonah or leave him be. Either way, you owe it to yourself to be whole and happy again. You have to do the work. No MaleForm can do it for you."

"You're so wise, Vivant. Too bad there aren't two of you. One could live here and the other could be my advisor on Revani."

When they laughed, it reminded Queen Vivant of when they were young.

"Two of me," said Queen Vivant. "Wouldn't that be something?"

Jacques's past

The enchanting Flames rose high above the hills, almost touching Space. Jacques walked slowly in front of the thousands of souls suffering within them.

Their hands stretched out, desperately begging him for mercy. Ignoring their cries for help, he found Lady Alarah rocking back and forth on her knees.

She was chanting an old Coldarian war song. It pleased him to see the Flames had driven her out of her mind.

"Rise, Lady Alarah, and face me."

She slowly looked up at him and frowned. "Who are you?"

"Stand, WomanForm. I don't answer to you."

He moved closer to the Flames.

"Would you like me to ease your suffering?"

She nodded eagerly. "Yes, please. Please quench the fire. It's unbearable!"

Circling a hand before the Flames, he willed them to be still. Learning a young King Anemi had received a bit of the Flames as a reward for helping another sorcerer escape from hell had piqued his interest.

After inheriting Platirius from his father, King Anemi used his dark magic to build the fiery prison to house souls, denying them access to The One's realm.

"I can release you. But...what will you do for me?"

"Anything," she panted. "Anything you want."

He smiled. "That's the correct answer."

S he tried not to look at the attractive MaleForm, but it was difficult. It had been quite a long while since she'd felt the comfort of one. He stared straight ahead as he steered the craft.

After nearly an hour had passed, he hadn't spoken. Her heart leapt into her throat when she saw a golden planet coming into view.

"Kikhani? Why are we going here? Why not take me to Coldarius?"

"Coldarius doesn't exist anymore," he said. "If you open your mouth one more time, I'll open the door and drop you into Space."

She quickly turned away and retrained her gaze on the golden magnificence of the palace. The craft dived before coming to a stop, hovering just outside the palace's gates.

"When you get out, ask for the ruler. Never mention you saw me or I'll kill you. Do you understand?"

Terrified, she looked at him and nodded.

"Tell me you understand!" he snarled.

"I understand! I won't tell anyone about you."

She recoiled from the contempt in his eyes.

"Good. Now get out."

When she leapt from the craft, it rose and sped off across the galaxy, leaving her to her fate. Eyeing her surroundings, she pulled the thin, satin hood over her head before making her way to the gate.

Before she could reach it, two female soldiers dressed in red armor came to greet her. Transfixed by what she saw, her steps slowed to a halt.

WomenForm soldiers? Impossible! Where are the MaleForms?

"Halt, WomanForm. You dare to trespass on Queen Revari's realm?"

"Who is Queen Revari?" she echoed. "I've never heard of her."

Swiftly, a sword was brought to her neck.

"I-I'm Lady Alarah of Coldarius! I come seeking asylum. May I please be brought to your king?"

The second soldier said, "Revani has no king, you fool!"

"But this is... Isn't this Kikhani?"

"We should kill you for your ignorance alone! Kikhani was conquered years ago and here you stand acting as if you're unaware of our queen's conquest!"

She roughly grabbed Lady Alarah by the arm and whirled her around to search her. After she was satisfied she wasn't carrying weapons, she nodded to the other soldier. "She's clean. Let's take her to—"

"I don't believe what I'm seeing."

The WomenForms turned and saw General Legend coming down the path. The soldiers saluted their commander.

General Legend stopped in front of Lady Alarah. "How is it possible you're here? I thought King Dubian had dealt with you years ago."

"Legend?" She took in the general's attire. "You're a soldier?"

"You will address our general appropriately," shouted the first soldier. "Do not question her as if you're her equal!"

General Legend never took her eyes off Lady Alarah. "I'll handle this, Private Carmen. I'm a general now, and that's how you'll refer to me."

I'm dreaming, thought Lady Alarah. *This is a terrible nightmare!*

"Forgive me, General Legend. I need to see your ruler, please."

General Legend smirked. "Oh, you do? And here I thought today would be boring. Follow me."

They entered the palace and walked for what seemed like an eternity before coming to an intricately carved crystal door inlaid with rubies and diamonds. General Legend scanned her hand across the TeleShield and entered, leaving Lady Alarah standing with the Revaltians.

A few minutes passed before the door buzzed open again. The soldiers led Lady Alara inside. Her eyes were wide with amazement at dozens of paintings and sculptures of a young queen who looked similar to—

"Queen Dellah!" she cried as Queen Revari approached her. Falling to her knees, she bowed with her face pressed into the floor. "Your Majesty! You're alive!"

Queen Revari stuck out her foot and kicked her. "Raise your head and face me, you dog!"

Whimpering, Lady Alarah did as she commanded. Something in the queen's eyes terrified her. She was Queen Dellah...but then...she wasn't. Surely she wasn't Queen Opal. Her clothes hadn't been so stylish.

"So you think I'm my mother?" She laughed. "I wish I had a diaper to throw at you."

"You're the baby I saw in the palace?!" exclaimed Lady Alarah.

When Queen Revari slightly tilted her head, General Legend handed her heavy BrainStaff to her. Without hesitation, she brought it down on Lady Alarah's head and beat her mercilessly while General Legend and the Revaltians looked on and laughed.

Unable to raise her arm anymore, she perused the bloodied and battered WomanForm at her feet. "That's for having the gall to address me so informally," said the queen. "How did you get here?"

"A...a MaleForm released me from the Flames," she whimpered.

"What MaleForm?!" roared the queen.

"I don't know, I swear it! He told me not to tell or he'd kill me."

160

Queen Revari laughed. "Do you believe you're safe here? Legend, give me my sword."

"Please, Your Majesty, I beg you!" begged Lady Alarah. "Please let me see my daughter one last time before you kill me!"

Cocking her head, Queen Revari lowered her sword. "Your daughter," she whispered. "Your daughter..."

Her chilling laugh frightened Lady Alarah more than anything she'd ever heard.

"The mother of General Lyric lying helpless in front of me. What have I done to deserve this stroke of luck?" She balanced her weight on the sword. "You know, I don't think I will kill you...yet. I've just thought of the perfect job for you. If you fail, I'll take my time removing your organs while you're still breathing. Have I been heard?"

"Yes, Your Highness! I'll do whatever you ask! I promise not to disappoint you!"

"Oh, I don't doubt that, Lady Alarah." The queen's eyes took on their signature red glow. "Disappointing me would be a grave mistake in judgment."

"**M**y King! We have a disturbance in the east wing!"

King Asa ran with the soldier to his visitor's bed chamber. He hurried through the doors to find the visitor attacking one of his best soldiers.

"Let him go!" he ordered.

He held a long blade to the sergeant's neck while one knee was firmly planted in his chest. Deeply offended, he said, "Why should I?"

King Asa looked into his crazed eyes and motioned for his soldiers to stand back. "I didn't bring you here to attack my troops!"

He had almost ordered all of Ziltach's prisoners to be killed, but his conscience prickled. It wasn't their fault they'd been on the receiving end of King Joaquin's sadistic ways. As he stared at the MaleForm, he felt something was wrong. Very wrong.

"Who are you?" asked King Asa.

The sergeant whimpered when he ran the blade across his neck.

"I'm Jacques! Who are you and where am I?"

"I'm King Asa and this is Onzi. My kingdom."

The blade barely moved again before a trickle of blood spilled down the sergeant's neck.

"How did I get here?"

"I brought you here from Ziltach. You've been here almost a year!"

His eyes sized up the king. "Are we your prisoners?"

"We?"

"Yes, Jonah, and everyone else you brought here."

162

King Asa held his breath. "I'm sorry, this is a bit...surprising."

Jacques cocked his head. "Not to me. All of you kings are the same. You want blood. You take and take, and never give! I'm not going to let anyone kill me!"

"There's no danger here. Ziltach has been absorbed into my realm. I'm keeping you...and Prince Jonah here until he's well enough to return to his family. He still has some...wild mannerisms."

Jacques tapped the soldier's face with the blade. "What happened to King Joaquin's soldiers?"

"They're dead. I have no use for barbarians walking around my realm, terrorizing my Beings. Please let my soldier go. He came to retrieve you for supper, not to die."

Without taking his eyes off King Asa, he lifted his knee from the soldier and tossed the blade to the ground. "Supper is the magic word."

K ing Asa watched him expertly slice into a large piece of beef roast with the cutlery. He took a sip of wine. "How did you end up on Ziltach?"

"I don't remember."

"Ah, I see. Do you have a home or family?"

Jacques poured more gravy on the roast and added a healthy scoop of creamed potatoes to his plate. "Not me, but Prince Jonah does. I'll go with him when he returns home."

Jacques held his stare. "I met Prince Jonah shortly after Princess Revari left for Earth. That's when he lost all hope. When he came to Ziltach, I stepped in to help him fight off the guards."

He took a swig of wine. "They wanted to do bad things to him, but I didn't let them. I skinned a few like rabbits. When they realized they couldn't defeat me, they moved on to torturing the weaker prisoners." He sank his teeth into the tender roast and said, "I kept him safe."

King Asa had his share of dealing with different Beings, but he'd never seen anyone like Jacques.

"I like Jonah," declared Jacques. "He's my friend. I'll protect him with my life."

"He's my friend too," said King Asa. "So where does that leave us?"

Jacques took a bite of pie. "If he tells me you've been good to him, then you and I will be friends too."

King Asa nodded. "Good. I've been assisting him to learn how to eat and speak properly again. I know his ParentForms are very worried about him. Now that General Kron has gone missing, they need him more than ever."

"His brother is gone? Where?"

"No one knows. Apparently, there was a battle on Saturn, but he never showed up and no one heard of the battle. It's very strange if you ask me."

"Very strange," said Jacques, forking up a bite of turnip greens. "Very strange indeed."

Dr. Barbara hurried up the hall to meet her next patient. She opened the door and found her sitting in her office.

Bowing, she said, "Queen Revari, thank you so much for coming. I hurried to get here when General Legend let me know you wanted to see me."

She sat down in front of the queen. "Thank you for trusting me. What may I help you with?"

She took in the doctor's brown suit, matching low heels, and no jewelry except a striking amethyst brooch pinned to her jacket. "It's not a matter of trust so much as wanting to move on with my life. When I was a ChildForm, I lived on Maieman with the Krons."

Dr. Barbara listened intently, copying notes on her palm where they could easily be erased. Once the queen became her patient, she'd record notes into her TranScreen.

"Although King Jonah swears I was happy, I don't remember a bit of it. Queen Marietta says my father kidnapped me and brought me back to Platirius, but my sister told me that's not true—she said I ran away from my SecondFamily."

She cleared her throat and looked around the room. For a moment, her stomach clenched as a wave of nausea swept over her. "I vaguely remember running away from Maieman. When a Platirian soldier found me, I had crossed the border between our realms. I was looking for Vivant."

"Do you remember why?"

She shook her head. "No. But I was crying and very frightened."

"What frightened you?"

She threw up her hands. "I don't know. Maybe I've been blocking whatever it is for a long time. I don't think I want to remember."

"The mind protects us from many things, Your Highness. It is our most powerful weapon against anything—even ourselves. I can help you remember your life on Maieman, but I'll caution you: sometimes, the past is better left buried. When we hide things from ourselves, it's for our own good. It's your choice if you'd like to move forward."

Queen Revari nodded her head. "Maybe you're right. Every time I try to remember, I get the worst headaches. Perhaps I'm not ready to know. I'm leaning toward what you said...my mind is being kind to me by keeping me in the dark."

She stood and adjusted a button on her black blazer. "Thank you, Dr. Barbara. If and when I feel the need to explore this, I'll return. For now, I'll be more open to new beginnings."

Dr. Barbara bowed to her again. "I'll be here when you need me, Your Majesty."

Queen Revari woke up to rain splattering against the windows. Turning to her husband, she said, "Oliver, Justin is crying. Get up."

"Hmmm..." he moaned.

"Oh, never mind. I'll get him."

She approached the baby's bassinet and reached for him before shrinking back in horror. An extremely malnourished baby looked up at her. Its mottled and wrinkled skin made her stomach churn.

"Help me!" he cried.

She screamed.

General Legend raced inside her bed chamber. "My Queen! What is it?"

Exhaling, she fell back on her pillows and stared up at the transparent ceiling. "Nothing, sister," she panted. "It was just a dream. A terrible one!"

"All right. I'm stationing two soldiers at your door. If you need me, I'll be right across the hall."

She turned toward the window. "Thank you, Legend. It's over now."

"Of course, Revari. Sleep well."

Yet sleep alluded her. She stared out at the moon, watching its iridescent brilliance change to blood red before her eyes. One by one, the stars disappeared from the sky, leaving an ominous vision of everything below it covered in blood.

Goosebumps appeared on her cold skin as waves of anxiety ripped through her mind. Something was coming. Something familiar and terrible. Instinctively, she shivered under the warm covers.

Epilogue

"Are you sure you want to keep this from King Jonah?" asked King Asa. "He has a lot invested in this too, you know."

Jacques stared out at the surfers trying to soar over high waves. They shouted with glee when the water washed them off the boards.

"Yes. He would try to stop me if he knew." He turned to King Asa. "I've always protected him with no questions asked. I wouldn't know how to take it if he reaches a point when he won't need me anymore."

"I think he'll always need you. He doesn't view life the way you do."

"He likes King Justin. I don't. He doesn't understand the threat a Human poses to us and our way of life. He has to go. There's no other choice."

King Asa nodded. "I agree. JanIus is very powerful. It doesn't deserve to be in his hands. If you killed him, then Revari would know who was behind it. And what of her? You know how Jonah feels about her."

"I do. I swear no harm will come to her. It's not something I expected, but I've fallen for her too. Jonah is so close to living the life he's always dreamed of. Everything will go according to plan. In time, she'll learn to live without her son."

King Jonah grabbed his head and moaned. The pounding headache he had was finally subsiding. As his vision cleared, he marveled at the figure standing in front of him.

"Asa?" He surveyed the white sands of the beach. "How the hell did we get out here?"

King Asa softly punched him on the arm. "You wanted to look at some of the property to purchase for Queen Revari, remember?"

The gaps in his memory were getting worse, but he trusted his friend.

"Of course. I think it'll be a nice surprise for her, don't you think?"

King Asa noticed a dark cloud replacing the sun. Night was coming fast. "I think," he said, "Queen Revari has a lot of surprises coming to her."

"Yes, I intend to make her so happy, she'll forget all about the hell she's experienced. We're almost there. Nothing will stand in our way now."

Deep within King Jonah's psyche, Jacques remained silent.

Author Bio

D.L. Hannah was born in Youngstown, Ohio. She is a writer, entrepreneur, and host of the Amerisogyny podcast. She is a Psi Chi and Alpha Kappa Delta member and earned a Bachelor of Arts degree in Clinical-Community Psychology from Walsh University. For over twenty years, she has been a strong advocate for children diagnosed with Autism. She now lives in North Carolina with her family.

Also by D.L. Hannah

Platirius: Infiltration Book I
Platirius: The Rise of Reve Book II
Platirius: Kikhani vs Platirius Book III
Coldarius: The Origin of Gallium Book I
Coldarius: The Betrayal Book II
JanIus: Pawns Book I
JanIus: Enter the King Book II
JanIus: Platirius vs JanIus Book III
Maieman: Paradox Book I
Maieman: Revelations Book II

www.ingramcontent.com/pod-product-compliance
Lightning Source LLC
Chambersburg PA
CBHW071914220626
47052CB00002B/350

* 9 7 8 1 9 6 5 7 9 8 2 8 7 *